Beau sat up and ~~...~~
Pressure filled h ~~...~~

Chloe slept like an angel, cuddled up against Aurora's chest, and Aurora's hand rested protectively on her back. Even in sleep they were both angels, for entirely different reasons. One had saved his soul, and the other was going to save his business.

Some of his movements must have awakened Aurora, because she took a breath and stirred. Her baby blues fluttered open, and she looked over at him with a sexy sleepiness he'd never imagined seeing in her eyes. At this moment he could just imagine waking up with her in his arms, taking his time to rouse her with kisses and caresses and sharing the morning with skin against skin.

When she looked into his eyes, still half-asleep, and smiled, he realized his body was trying to take him down a road he didn't want to go. At least not yet.

Dear Reader,

Thank you very much for reading my latest book! This is a very special one as it is set in my hometown. Some changes have been made to suit the story, but the essence of the area is still true.

Readers and friends from here have been asking to have our little hometown as a setting for one of my stories and so I finally did it. Some of the characters are named after childhood friends, and my mother even has a character named after her. The town I grew up in is in rural western Pennsylvania, where there are more cows than people, no sidewalks, and it's miles from the nearest store. As a child, much of my time was spent in the woods, at the lake or catching fireflies on long summer evenings. During the winters I spent hours reading books, which fostered my love of a good story and the desire to write my own.

I have many fond memories of growing up in this community, and I wanted to share them with my readers. If you are so moved, drop me an email at mollyevansromance@gmail.com and let me know what you're up to, what you might like to see in a future story or tell me a story of your own. After all, all good books start with a good story.

Regards,

Molly Evans

A MOMMY FOR
HIS BABY

———

MOLLY EVANS

ISBN-13: 978-0-373-21509-6

A Mommy for His Baby

First North American Publication 2017

Copyright © 2017 by Brenda Hampton

Printed in U.S.A.

Books by Molly Evans

Harlequin Medical Romance

The Greek Doctor's Proposal
One Summer in Santa Fe
Children's Doctor, Shy Nurse
Socialite…or Nurse in a Million?
Her Family for Keeps
Safe in the Surgeon's Arms

Visit the Author Profile page
at Harlequin.com for more titles.

**Praise for
Molly Evans**

"This was a well-written Medical Romance set in New Mexico and it moves in a fast and exciting pace."

—*Goodreads* on
Her Family for Keeps

CHAPTER ONE

WHAT HAD POSSESSED Aurora Hunt to return to this little town, she didn't know. She should have figured out on her own how to survive, how to find a new job, how to create a new life. Somehow. But after being beaten down by life during several unforeseeable events she'd given up, given in, and gone home to her childhood home in western Pennsylvania to lick her wounds. Wounds that scarred her on the inside as well as the outside.

Nothing in this vast wilderness settled in the heart of the Appalachian Mountains had changed much in two hundred years. The car models were newer, farmers plowed different fields, and there were more houses built on what had once been pasture. At the heart of it, its people, their culture, hadn't changed—had refused to change—and that was why she'd left in the first place. In order to grow, things had to change, and she'd wanted to do all of that where there were more opportunities than in this remote village.

But due to a nearly catastrophic car wreck, she was back to square one. In one second, one dramatic turn of the wheel, her life had taken a path she'd never expected and she'd been forced to move in with her mother.

For now.

This situation was only temporary. Until she regained her strength and figured out what she was going to do with her life. A few weeks, tops. Living with her mother on a permanent basis was *not* an option.

Getting out of her car wasn't as easy as getting into it. Nearly every movement she made was difficult, but she was grateful for the pain. At least it meant she was still alive, still moving forward. Nothing was what it had used to be. Nothing.

Today she was calling on an old friend to help put her life back together, one aching bone at a time.

The sign for the local medical clinic was a red arrow, pointing to a door. Until a few months ago there had been no medical clinic in Brush Valley. The closest one had been miles away. So it was understandable that this building didn't quite look like it was a thriving business just yet.

It looked like the building had once belonged to an animal doctor instead of a people doctor. Faded paint indicated dogs to the left, cats to the right. She didn't know which one to take, but since she was more of a dog person she entered through the left door. Fortunately both doors opened into the lobby of the clinic, which was nearly deserted.

"Good morning, can I help you?" A woman in an advanced stage of pregnancy smiled and offered her a clipboard to sign in.

"Yes. I have an appointment."

"Okay, great." She looked at Aurora's name, then frowned. "Are you related to *Sally* Hunt?"

"Yes, she's my mother."

"Oh, then you must have grown up here!" She held out her hand. "I'm Cathy Carter. I think I went to school just after you."

"Oh…great to meet you."

Though Aurora didn't recall everyone who had gone to school around the time she had, the woman did look vaguely familiar, with her big brown eyes and long brown hair.

"I'm sure you don't remember me." She patted her belly. "I looked much different back then."

That made Aurora laugh. "Didn't we all? Nice to see you again."

"Have a seat and he'll be with you in a few

minutes. Just one patient ahead of you." Cathy nodded to a young woman with a sniffling infant, pacing the small waiting room.

"No problem."

"Angie, why don't you bring Zachary back and we'll have a look at him now?" Laboriously, Cathy rose from the chair and followed the mom and baby into the first exam room.

Aurora felt sorry for the woman, who looked like she was carrying a watermelon beneath her clothing. But although Cathy looked uncomfortable, she also looked happy, and there was something to be said about that.

While Aurora waited she paced the length of the waiting room as sitting caused her too much pain. As she moved back and forth, trying to keep her joints moving, she noticed a bulletin board, with notices for parents, and a table full of retirement magazines. There was a section of toys for little kids, but nothing for anyone else. It was a sparse attempt to keep those who were waiting entertained. These days, with all the electronic devices and people being plugged in, the corner looked lacking, without at least one charger available.

"Aurora?" Cathy called her to the desk. "I can take you back and get you in a patient room, take your vitals, while Beau—I mean Dr. Gutterman—looks at his other patient."

"Oh, you can call him Beau. I know when we're behind the desk we all go on a first-name basis."

"That's right. You're a nurse, too, aren't you?"

"Well, yes." At least she *had* been. She didn't want to say that she wasn't a nurse any longer. Just because she was in between jobs at the moment. "I'm not working right now—but I guess once a nurse, always a nurse, right?"

"Yes, we're kind of like the Marines that way."

Cathy led the way and indicated a nice patient room. After a quick check, she left Aurora waiting for Beau.

"Leave the door open, please. I get a little claustrophobic."

"Oh, sure. He'll be right here." Cathy pressed a hand to her back as a twinge of pain crossed her face.

"Are you okay?"

"Yes. It's just pushing on my back more and more the last few days."

"Oh, boy. When are you due?" That low back pain was an ominous sign. Labor could commence at any moment.

"A few more weeks—but I'm feeling like I want to pop right now." Cathy paused in the doorway and looked like she was about to pass out. "I've been having Braxton Hicks for days."

Feeling that nurse's instinct kick in, Aurora quickly moved to Cathy's side and began to assess the woman. Maternity wasn't her specialty, but she could see the swelling in the woman's hands and face, the flushed cheeks and the fine sheen of sweat on her face and neck.

"Cathy, I'm not so sure they were false contractions. I think you'd better sit down."

"I do, too."

Without releasing her grip on Cathy's arm, Aurora dragged one of the wheeled chairs in the room close, right behind the pregnant woman's legs. "Here's a chair."

"Oh, boy." Cathy dropped into the chair, then clutched her abdomen and leaned forward with a groan. "I think I'm going into labor right now."

She blew out a breath and her face reddened further.

"Oh. Oh, *no*! My water just broke."

The amniotic fluid housing the baby and adding cushioning splattered onto the floor. This was going to go hard and fast.

"Let me call for Beau."

Aurora left the room for a second to dash across the hall and rap on the patient room door.

"Dr. Gutterman—there's an issue out here!"

Beau jerked the door open with a scowl, then a surprised look raised his brows and a grin lit up his face. "Aurora! What are you—?"

"Cathy's going into labor. *Now*." Trying not to panic, Aurora released the doorknob.

"Oh! I knew she was close, but not that close." Beau turned back to his patient's mother. "I'm sorry, Angie. I'll call in a prescription for Zach as soon as I can. Give me a call if he's not better in a few days."

Dispensing with any more pleasantries or greetings, Aurora grabbed his arm and dragged him into the hallway. "I mean *right* now."

"Oh! I see."

Beau headed into the other patient room. He looked at his nurse, struggling against pain in the office chair.

"Oh, boy. I haven't delivered a baby in a long time." He offered a quick glance to Aurora, his eyes wide. "Are you *sure* she's going to have it right now?"

"Yes," Aurora said as Cathy screamed again.

"We'd better call 911."

"Do it—but you may be delivering a baby before they get here. This looks precipitous."

Though Aurora had done several rotations in Delivery, she hadn't attended a birth in some time—and this one was looking like it was going to be a doozy.

"No! I don't want to have it here. I can't!" Cathy huffed her breath in and out, her doe eyes wide in fear as she looked at Aurora for help. "We have *plans*."

"Honey, those plans are about to go up in smoke," Aurora said. "Where's your husband?"

"Home."

"You'd better call him," Aurora said, and watched as Beau called the emergency services to send an ambulance as soon as possible. Out in the country, nothing was "stat", or "fast," as they were miles from everywhere.

"Okay. Okay…" Cathy took a deep breath and leaned back in the chair as the pain obviously eased. She held the phone to her ear. As she looked at Aurora for reassurance another frown crossed her face and she took a deep breath. "Honey? The baby's coming!"

Aurora took the phone before Cathy crushed it to pieces in her hand. "Your wife is at the clinic and she's in labor. You'd better get here quickly if you want to see your baby being born."

Then she hung up. He'd either get there or he wouldn't. Aurora's first priority was to see this woman and her baby safe.

"Cathy, we've got to get you ready to have this baby."

"What about the ambulance?" She rose from the chair with Beau and Aurora's help, leaning heavily on both of them.

"You know as well as I do that it'll take them half an hour to get here, and you're going to have this baby long before that."

Beau ripped off his lab coat and rolled up his sleeves, then scrubbed his hands and arms vigorously at the sink, jumping into the mode necessary to save both his nurse and her baby.

He knew heroes weren't born. They were made. In situations like this.

"Aurora—good to see you, my friend, but it looks like we're going to be welcoming a baby in the next few minutes. Are you up to it?"

"Absolutely." There was nothing, not even the pain in her back, that would interfere with her ability to save a life or two today.

"Great. Let's get her on the exam table and see what's going on."

His jaw was tense, and he didn't look at Aurora as he scrubbed. When his child had been born his wife had died. That was all she knew. The shock of this unforeseen delivery was obviously stirring that memory. Was he struggling to push it aside? Until now she hadn't thought of that, and her heart ached for him. Those memories had to be incredibly painful for him, but he was mustering through and doing what was needed in the moment.

"Oh, no. *Oh, no.*" Cathy bent at the waist and

clutched her abdomen, nearly crushing Aurora's fingers. *"Agh!"*

"Beau, I don't think the table is going to work. It's not designed for this. How about we put some blankets and sterile sheets on the floor and let her squat, like she seems to want to?"

"Okay. Good idea." Beau grabbed blankets and two sterile packages.

Together she and Beau turned the room into an impromptu delivery suite. This was so over the top of what she'd expected to be doing today, but knowing there were no other options, and that Beau had her back, she had his—she knew they could do it together.

"Do you have a surgical kit around in case we need it?" Chewing her lip for a second, Aurora didn't want to think about the possibility of having to do an emergency C-section, but planning for the worst and hoping for the best had always worked for her.

"Yes—there." Beau pointed to another cupboard over the sink. "It's a general kit. Everything we need should be in it."

"Breathe, Cathy. Just breathe." Aurora tried to keep her voice calm and not let the woman know about the anxiety pulsing through her body. "I'm going to reach around you and remove your shoes and leggings."

"Okay." Cathy nodded. "It's easing now." She

took in a few deep breaths, sweat pouring off of her. "Beau, you aren't going to fire me because I had my baby in your office, are you?"

Beau barked out a laugh and gave her a comforting pat on the shoulder, the light in his eyes not as dark as it had been a few moments ago. "No. Although I do have to say it's going to go down as one of the most interesting days I've ever had."

"That's *g-o-o-o-o-d*!" Another contraction hit, nearly dropping Cathy to her knees.

"Let's get you down before you fall." Aurora tucked a hand on Cathy's waist and eased her to her knees, then sat her back so that Beau could check and see if the baby was crowning.

A door slammed in the front office.

"We have company."

"Cathy? *Cathy!* Where are you?" Hurried footsteps got closer to the room.

"We're in the back, Ron!" Beau yelled toward the door.

"Oh, my God. You *are* in labor. It wasn't a joke." Ron, clearly Cathy's husband, stood in the doorway, panting from his exertion, his eyes wide as he took in the scene. "I can't believe it."

"No jokes today. Wash your hands over there," Aurora pointed to the sink. "This is going to go fast."

"She's definitely crowning," Beau said after he had a quick look.

"He. It's a he. I know it." Cathy began to pant again. "Oh, here he comes! I have to push again—get me up!"

Cathy struggled to a sitting position, then Beau and Ron helped her to her knees. With one hand she held onto her husband, with the other she clutched the edge of the patient table.

"Go with it, Cathy. Wait until you can't wait any longer and then push."

"I'm pushing *now*!" Her statement ended in a scream, a gasp, then another push.

"He's almost here," Beau said from his position on the floor nearby. He placed a sterile cloth beneath the baby's head and supported it. "Pant. I need to check the cord."

Cathy cast tear-filled eyes at her husband, who looked like he'd been hit by a truck. "Honey? We're having a baby today!"

"I… I can see that." He looked down at his wife and pressed a kiss to her cheek. "Wasn't quite what I was expecting, though."

"Me, either. Oh! Pushing again."

"Go ahead. One more ought to do it."

With a great groan, Cathy pushed the vernix-covered baby into Beau's waiting hands.

"Ron? Can you help me sit her back?" Pain

was slicing through Aurora's back and she couldn't do it alone.

"Yes."

Together they eased Cathy into a reclining position, supported by her husband's chest. Exhausted, Cathy drew in cleansing breaths and closed her eyes.

"We have to do a few things, then you can hold your baby."

Beau's voice, choked with emotion, drew her attention. He focused, he did the job, but she could see the pain in his face. Tears pricked Aurora's eyes at the miracle of birth that had happened so unexpectedly right in front of her, but she shoved them back. Now wasn't the time to think of the family that she'd wanted and never been able to have. Might never have. Beau was struggling with his own issues and had set them aside. So could she.

"You were right, Cathy. It's a boy. He's perfect."

Beau provided the news, the tension in the room eased, and Aurora was able to take a deep breath, too.

"All parts are there, and exactly where they belong."

He finished wiping the baby's face, then Aurora used a suction bulb to clean out his mouth and nose and placed him in his mother's arms.

"I can't believe this! We delivered a baby today." Beau gave a laugh and shook his head, some of the emotion leaving his face and his shoulders relaxing.

"I can't either," Cathy said, with tears flowing down her face as she looked at her baby, then leaned into her husband's neck.

"How did this happen?" Ron asked. "I thought you weren't due for two more weeks."

"Well, your son had other plans."

"I can certainly see that." He let out a shaky breath and with one trembling finger touched his son's hand. "I just can't believe this." He held out his hand. "I'm shaking. Nothing *ever* gets to me, but I'm shaking like a leaf."

"Well, this circumstance is very different than anything else you've ever experienced, isn't it?"

It wasn't every day that a new dad had to come screeching into the parking lot of his wife's place of work to see his baby being born.

"You're right about that." He blew out a breath and shook his head, letting out a tremulous laugh. "You are *definitely* right about that."

The front door opened again, to admit the ambulance crew with their stretcher and equipment.

"Did we miss the party?" A leggy brunette paramedic stuck her head into the room, offering a cheery grin, but her observant dark eyes were looking for anything that was out of place.

"You sure did. It was a doozy, too." Aurora shook her head, still in shock at the day's events.

"Aurora...?" the paramedic said, and frowned as if she were trying to figure something out. "Is that really you? I haven't seen you in years! It's *Missy*!"

The woman who had gone to high school with Aurora held her arms out and embraced her.

"Missy—hi! Yeah. It's me." She gave a nervous laugh. This was turning into quite a day of friends from her past showing up unexpectedly. "It was a trip I hadn't really planned. But here I am. It's great to see you."

"You, too. Everyone okay?" Missy asked. Those eyes of a trained observer looked around the room again, focusing on the mom and baby.

"I think so—but they're going to need a trip to the hospital for a full exam." Beau stripped his gloves off and tossed them on the growing pile of trash.

"You got it. Sirens or no sirens?" Missy gave a smile and a wink.

"No sirens today." Beau shook his head and gave an amazed laugh. "Wow!"

Cathy reached out to Beau and he stepped forward and clasped her hand. "Beau. I hate to ask this right now, but can I have my maternity leave starting today?"

Everyone laughed at the absurd request.

"Of course you can. It's not a problem. But I'll miss you, and I just hope I don't destroy the place while you're gone."

"You won't. You'll be fine."

"Six weeks, right?"

"Yes. I'll let you know if it needs to be longer." She cast a loving eye on her husband and her baby as tears filled her eyes. "This has been such an amazing event, I'm not sure I'm going to want to come back."

"Don't talk like that." Beau squeezed her fingers again and shook Ron's hand. "Just keep me updated and let me know when you're ready to come back." He snorted. "*If* you are."

"I will. I promise."

"Ready now?" Missy asked.

"Ready." Cathy sighed and clutched the baby securely in both arms.

After mother and baby had been packed onto the stretcher and were headed to the hospital Aurora and Beau faced each other, alone for the first time since the event had begun. For a few seconds they stared at each other, unblinking, then Aurora laughed.

The tension-reliever caught her by surprise,

and she clasped her hands to her face. "*Beau!* We delivered a *baby*!"

"I know—I was here." A grin split his face and he held his arms wide. "Now that all the excitement is over, let's have a proper greeting. Come here."

"I don't think I can walk after that. My legs are shaking."

But she had enough strength to close the gap, and Beau met her halfway.

"You held it together during a crisis—the sign of a true professional, right? That's the most important part." He closed his long arms around her and squeezed.

CHAPTER TWO

THE SURGE OF adrenaline and attraction that pulsed through her was completely unexpected in the embrace of an old friend she hadn't seen in ten years.

Her heart did a little flip at the sight of his long, sun-bleached blond hair that had a tendency to fall into his eyes, and the strength in that jaw she hadn't remembered being so masculine. Memories of the past, of her secret crush on him, surged forward, and she hesitated a second, trying to breathe through the onslaught of unanticipated emotions suddenly swirling within her.

Wow. She certainly hadn't expected *this* reaction.

Though she'd sworn off men after her recent painful break-up, her hormones obviously hadn't taken the same oath.

Clearing her throat, she reined in those wandering senses of hers that appreciated a fine-looking man. Now wasn't the time to be ogling anyone—let alone a good friend—no matter how broad those shoulders were.

She returned the embrace, trying not to gasp in pain. The strength of his arms, the pressure of his hug closed in on her, lighting up the injuries in her back like an electrical grid. A groan of discomfort escaped her throat.

"Did I hurt you?" He pulled back, his green eyes assessing, concern evident, and ran his gaze over her face, trying to determine what had happened.

"I'm sorry. I'm in quite a lot of pain right now—which is why I'm here to see you in the first place."

Back to her original goal: to be pain and medication-free, to get her life back in order. Starting now.

"Pain? You hid it well during this whole thing." He released her and gave her one gentle pat on the shoulder.

"Probably an adrenaline surge got me through."

He lifted one hand and indicated that she walk ahead of him into the nearby patient room. "You're my last patient of the day, so we can take our time—have a look at you and do some catching up." The dark brows over his green eyes lowered, pinning her with a direct look. "Tell me what's going on."

"I'll give you the short version. Car wreck. Lots of back pain. I want to get off the pain medications."

The last few months had been beyond brutal. A severe car crash had ripped her life and her relationship apart. Every time she told the story the pain surfaced—the emotional pain she'd gone through as well as the physical pain which was the reason for her visit today.

She handed him a folder with copies of her medical records. "The long version is in here. If you don't mind, read it later. Right now I just want to see if you can help me with the pain."

That was short, sweet and to the point. Rehashing her past wasn't going to help her today. Telling him about the fight with her boyfriend— the reason for her car accident—was going to have to wait. The end of their relationship had come soon after the crash, due to her physical scars, and had destroyed her.

"That doesn't sound very good." He harrumphed and placed the manila folder aside and focused on her. "I'll take a look at that later, for sure. Right now I want to look at *you*."

"Thanks, Beau. I'm sorry, but I *hate* this pain. Every time I move something hurts, and then if I stay still too long I get stiff."

The pain receded slightly as she walked along beside him, but the memory of it lingered.

"I can't win."

Tears pricked her eyes, but she pushed them back. Tears hadn't been tolerated by her father, so she'd learned to suppress her emotions. Even now she had difficulty sharing them.

"You certainly can win—but winning may look a little different than you thought. You were in a serious crash. Getting through an experience like that takes time." They entered the patient room. "Did you go through any physical therapy?"

"Yes. Two months of inpatient rehab. They said they did everything they could, but there's got to be something else."

Tears filled her eyes—tears she'd thought she'd finished shedding. Desperation circled her heart and squeezed hard. The pressure in her chest of the emotional pain focused there was like talons, digging in and not letting go.

"Though you did go through some rehabilitation, there's still work to be done. Rehab facilities often focus on one modality, not on being open to other adjunctive aspects of care that can help people just as much as the traditional ways."

"Really?" That statement perked her up. Somehow, deep in her gut, she knew there *had* to be alternative treatments, but she just didn't know what.

"You came to the right place."

The look in his eyes caused a surge of warmth through her. Hope pulsed in her chest. With the help of this man—her friend—she knew she was going to get through this tough time.

He peered at her with those intense green eyes that perfectly fit his streaked blond hair. He wouldn't look out of place with a surfboard tucked under one arm and hanging out on the beach. Except there wasn't a beach for three hundred miles.

"I'm so glad. You don't know what a relief it is to hear that."

Struggling with her emotions, she swallowed twice before she could speak again.

"It was awful. Having doctors telling me I'd never walk again, accept it. I think their sympathies ran out at the same time my insurance benefits did."

She clutched her hands together to stop their trembling. The memory of the accident had faded somewhat, but she still felt the aftereffects.

"I'm trying not to think too much about that part of it. I'm moving forward, working on my physical abilities, but the pain is so intense at times I can hardly move."

"You are one tough lady, Aurora—but you always have been."

Beau pressed his hand against hers, this time offering comfort with a simple touch, and she appreciated the gesture.

"I can see you're in pain. I'm a D.O.—Doctor of Osteopathy—and I perform manipulations of the body in addition to running the straight-up medical practice. That's probably a little different than you're used to."

"Yes, it is, but I'll consider anything that will get me where I want to be."

"Where *is* that? What's your goal?" The smile he gave lifted one side of his mouth, making him look like he had a secret.

"I want to be pain-free, off the medications, and back to my old self again. There has to be a way other than just taking more pills or different pills."

What a relief, a joy, a gift it would be to have her old life back. Or at least to have her body back so she could take the rest of her life where she wanted it to go.

Right now she didn't even know where that was. Working in a hospital again might not ever be possible due to her injury. Her job was on hold, her apartment had been packed up and put in storage… She looked at her friend, hoping he could really give her the help she needed when no one else had been able to.

"There's always another way—no matter what the issue is." Beau went on to describe several natural methods of pain control. "Massage would work. Yoga would be helpful, gentle, and it would provide the flexibility you need."

"Yoga? I never thought of that." She sighed as relief started to form in her mind. "I have to be back in action as soon as possible or my mother is going to drive me nuts."

That was something Beau couldn't do anything about. Her relationship and her problems with her mother were long term and would probably never change.

"How so?" He opened up a computer program, typing as they talked.

"I moved into her house with the intention of staying just a few days, until I can really figure out what I'm going to do. Unfortunately she's determined to be my nurse, psychotherapist and nutritionist instead of my mother."

Yeah, it was all or nothing with her. Always had been. Always would be. At her mother's age, there would be no changing her.

Yet another reason she'd left home at such an early age. While growing up Aurora had felt like she'd been hatched or adopted. She hadn't felt as if she belonged to her family. They'd had very distinct ideas on what she should be and what she should do with her life that hadn't matched at all with what *she'd* wanted. *Her* needs, her wants, her dreams, had been squashed by her family.

The only solution she'd been able to come to had been to leave. To get away. Forge a life for herself elsewhere. So she'd broken out and left the state to fulfill her career goals at a large university hospital in Virginia.

At least she'd gotten that part right. A husband and family of her own had been more elusive.

Being in charge of her life was something that she would never change. But those ideas of building a life with someone, having a family, had begun to surface—then had crashed into oblivion after the breakup with her boyfriend and the car wreck. Eventually she'd figured out that he wasn't a long-term kind of guy. Wasn't in it for the long haul and didn't have the fortitude to be the man she needed.

The first time he'd seen her scars he'd recoiled. That had been the end for both of them. All the plans she'd made for her future had come crashing down and she'd come home to Brush Valley to lick her wounds, heal, and recover from the accident and the breakup.

Here she was. Home again. Starting over. A new Aurora, reinventing her life.

Beau looked at her for a moment, contemplating. "I'm sure your mother was scared when you were hurt, right? She's probably not over the shock of it, so you'll have to cut her a break a while longer."

That thought *had* occurred to Aurora, and she dropped her eyes away from the intensity of him, the truth in his words. "I know, and I appreciate her efforts, but if I hang around the house all the time she'll feel compelled to wait on me. It won't be good for either of us."

Beau lifted his hands and looked around, as if suddenly struck by a bold new idea. "Well, as you know, I'm suddenly without a nurse and I need one immediately. I would *love* to have you help out as much as you can. If you'd be interested in working with me, that is?"

"What? Really?"

She hadn't thought of working while she was in Brush Valley, let alone working with Beau. She hadn't let her mind wander in that direction, but now it seemed like a great idea.

Her heart thrummed in anticipation, her throat constricted for a few seconds, and then her eyes widened. "I couldn't work full-time yet, but I can answer phones, make patient appointments and work the triage line for you."

The stress would be way less than working in the hospital, so she might be able to swing it. Could this be the answer she needed?

"What triage line?" Beau gave a sideways smile, lifting one corner of his mouth. "I bought the building a year ago...right before Chloe was born. A lot has happened since then, and I haven't gotten everything in place." He shook his head, but there was a smile there. "Maybe you can help me get caught up."

"That would be fantastic! I could start any time. Like tomorrow."

The idea of working with Beau, helping to get his business going and refilling her bank account were both very appealing.

"This would solve so many of my problems—just like that." She snapped her fingers.

"For me, too. Agency nurses are hard to find this far out in the country, and I hadn't even thought of looking for one yet because Cathy still had a couple weeks before she was due." He snorted and shook his head, his eyes wide in self-deprecation. "Underestimated *that* one, big-time. But, if you're serious, can you really start tomorrow?"

"Absolutely." Joy lifted her mood immeasurably. "My temporary disability payments run out in a week, so working for you will be the

perfect answer until I can figure out a more permanent solution."

"Deal. You're hired." He looked away for a
second, then back at her. "Do you want to return
to Virginia and your job there? Or are you considering something else? You've been missed
around here. By everyone."

The look he gave her was pointed, and guilt
filled the empty space in her gut. The people
around here had once been her friends, her family, and she'd left them behind in order to have
a life for herself elsewhere. Now...? Who knew
what the future held, but returning here permanently hadn't crossed her mind.

A sigh tumbled out of her throat. "I just don't
know. With hospital work there's always a lot
of lifting and pulling and tugging of patients or
beds or equipment." Her shoulders drooped as
saying the words aloud made them more real. "I
couldn't physically do the job right now, which
is really disappointing."

"All the years you spent training and gaining experience feel like they're going down the
drain?"

Somehow, he'd hit it right on the head.

"Yes. Maybe it's not true, but at this moment
it sure feels like it."

Sadness, grief for her loss, overwhelmed her
for a second. She'd left this small town to cre-

ate a life for herself, and now that life had been
changed dramatically the first thing she'd done
was head home—back to Brush Valley, where
she knew she could recover. Could she leave
again so quickly? It felt like a betrayal to think
of leaving again and it made her very uncomfortable.

"So, be objective for a few minutes. What
would you tell a patient if they were in your
position?"

"I don't want to play this game, Beau." Being
vulnerable was hard for her. Being vulnerable
in front of Beau was even worse.

"That's because you know I'm right. What
I'm trying to do is get you to think outside of
your pain. Come on—humor me. What would
you tell a patient? If it helps, consider this a job
interview question."

Huffing out a sigh, Aurora closed her eyes
for a moment, thinking, then opened them and
looked at Beau. "I would tell a patient that this is
a moment in time, and not to make any big decisions while still recovering, to relax about it."

"Perfect!" He patted her on the knee. "Now
you know exactly what I was going to advise
you."

He twitched his brows once at her and a smile
found its way to her lips.

"Fine. You're right. I'll hold off on making

any big decisions. At least for now. I'll work with you and we'll see how it goes, how my back does, and what other opportunities arise for my future—what I want to do, where I want to live."

Saying it like that, all in a rush, sounded reasonable, but it was so hard to accept. Time marched on while she stood still. At least it seemed that way.

Maybe all she needed was a little more time, and Beau was right about that. Being driven, focusing on accomplishing her goals in life, had gotten her places. Having her goals and her life stalled due to injury was *not* the way she wanted to live. Doing nothing was incredibly frustrating.

"Good idea. Speaking of living situations, you mentioned your mom…? Think you'll be okay there?"

Having lived alone for years, she valued her private space. "Although I love my mom, I can't stay with her for long. Do you know of anyone with a room for rent? It doesn't have to be much."

"As a matter of fact there's a small apartment upstairs you can use for free. It's not fancy, but it would give you some privacy, and it's a short commute down the stairs to work."

He winked and some of the tension in her eased.

"I was going to rent it out eventually. For now, consider it one of the perks of working for me."

"Oh, Beau. That would be fantastic." Could this day get any better? "I would *love* that. And as my finances improve, I can pay some rent."

This was the first time in ages she'd felt so excited about anything. Allowing hope to find a place in her heart had been an exercise in disappointment over the last months. Maybe now, maybe here, the time had come to take it out for a stroll.

"You'll get turned around in no time. For now, I'm not going to worry about it. It doesn't cost me anything for you to live there." He waved away her protest. "What are friends for, anyway?"

"I can't thank you enough. Just know that as soon as I can I'll pay you back. I don't want to owe you any more than I have to."

"You're a qualified pediatrics nurse, if I remember correctly—right?"

"Yes, but currently a semi-disabled one."

That fact irritated her. Depending on others for jobs and apartments wasn't the way she wanted to live her life. She'd made her own way in life since she'd graduated college.

"Semi-disabled *temporarily*." He held up her

file, then set it aside. "What's contained in that file isn't all of who you are. Remember, it's a bump in the road and we'll get you over it—or around it—one way or another. For now consider the apartment as part of your pay." He picked up the file again and read a few lines. "According to your doctors you've made excellent progress."

A snort of derision escaped her throat. "According to *them*, but it's not enough for *me*. It won't be until I get my life back."

A grin split his face, lighting up his eyes and adding a sparkle to them she'd hadn't yet seen today.

"Knowing you, you won't be satisfied until you're swinging from the rafters in your dad's barn."

That made her laugh—a genuine feeling that surfaced from deep within her, eliciting memories that hadn't seen the light of day for years. The pleasure bubbled up from her chest and burst out of her. This expression of joy was unfamiliar. The last few months had been brutal. A good laugh was definitely called for today.

She wiped her eyes with the heels of her hands and took in a tremulous breath. "I guess you're right. Those were good times, weren't they?"

"They sure were."

A haunted look flashed through his eyes. She'd seen fatigue in the lines of his face, how he rubbed his eyes when he thought no one was looking, and the look of pain when he'd handed the newborn baby to Cathy. Although she knew that his wife had died, she didn't know all of the circumstances.

"You said the office is new, but I guess I didn't realize how new your practice really is."

Changing the topic away from things that were too personal for both of them seemed like a good idea. Now that she'd be working with him there would be plenty of time to get reacquainted. Right now she needed pain relief.

"After working for someone else in a large city clinic I figured out pretty quickly that it wasn't for me. So I broke out on my own, bought the building and got it ready for business." He winked and gave that charming grin of his. "I like to run the ship, not swab the decks. At this point in my life building my own business the way I want it seems like the way to go."

The tension in the air that had been rising between them evaporated. They were back to an easy back and forth banter which eased her mind as well as some of the knots in her back.

"That doesn't surprise me." She looked around. "This seems more like you than working at a large clinic. I think you're better suited to a rural setting, where you know your patients, than having huge numbers of patients run through your office every day." She shrugged. "Not you. At least in my opinion."

"Yes, you're exactly right. I'm just getting going here, but I have high expectations. People have told me for years that Brush Valley needs a health clinic, so now we have one."

Though he was saying the right words, there didn't seem to be much passion in him—for them or for his new business venture.

"It's a good thing. Maybe it will inspire more people to start businesses, too."

"Then why do you look like hell?"

"That's one thing I love about you, Aurora— you shoot straight and tell it like it is." He gave a chuckle, but the laughter didn't extend all the way to his eyes. "I appreciate it that you didn't tell me I look worse than that."

"You look like you haven't slept in a year." There was something going on with him—more than just running a new business.

"You're almost right."

He shoved a hand through his hair and his eyes darkened for a moment. The fun-loving Beau she'd known had had some hard times recently.

"Seriously?" She blinked, startled by the answer. "That's a long time to go without a good night's sleep."

He nodded, his face grim. "It's been a rough year." He rubbed a hand over his face.

"Is it something you want to talk about?" She leaned forward, then cringed when her back tightened at the movement.

"You know that I have a child? A daughter… Chloe."

"Oh, I see. If *she* doesn't sleep, you don't either?" She smiled. That explained a lot. In her pediatrics experience she'd heard that story many times from parents.

"Yes, well… Julie…my wife…died right after Chloe was born, so it's always been just the two of us." He dropped his gaze and cleared his throat, then picked up Aurora's file from the desk again.

"Beau, I'm so sorry. Do you have someone to help you?"

Surely he wasn't trying to cope with everything all by himself. Everyone needed help—especially in a situation like this. Grief for him cramped her heart. He had to be in such pain. No wonder he wasn't sleeping.

Instead of answering her question, he looked away and cleared his throat. "How about for now we focus on you? We can talk about the disaster of my personal life another time."

"Okay. Sure." Now she reached out and placed her hand over his. As she did so the simple movement stirred a hot, burning sensation from her wrist to her hip. "Oh! Ow." She cringed, unable to hide the grimace on her face.

"You really *do* need some body work done, don't you?"

"Body work?" Her eyes went wide, then she frowned. "What does *that* mean?"

"Manipulation and massage."

"Then let's get to it."

"Let's get you into the treatment room and I'll see what I can do."

CHAPTER THREE

WHEN AURORA LEFT the clinic an hour later she was walking straight for the first time in months and she could take a deep breath of the fresh Pennsylvania air without pain. Awesome. All because of Beau.

For the first time since the crash she had hope. Beau had given that back to her.

After making the drive to her mother's house, Aurora stepped through the door to the fragrance of her mother's cooking. Instantly she was transported back to when her mother had given her cooking lessons as a child, when she'd had to stand up on a stool to reach the counter and the stove. Those were lessons she'd hated at the time, but she used them almost every day now. *Go figure.*

"Mom? Where are you?"

"In the kitchen."

Walking through the living room to the kitchen, Aurora began to feel the stiffness that Beau had warned her about. She wanted to lean back on an ice pack, the way he'd recommended, and read on the couch for a while. Reading had saved her life as a kid, during the long Pennsylvania winters, and she hadn't done nearly enough of it in the last few years. Today seemed like a good time to catch up a little, but first there was the task of telling her mother she was moving out.

"What are you making? It smells great." Steam wafted up from every pot on the stove and a blast of heat caught her in the face.

"Making beef stew for dinner. It's better if it simmers all day." Sally looked at her daughter. "You didn't forget that, did you?"

"No, I remember." Her stomach growled in response to the fragrance. "Guess I need to eat something *now*, though."

Opening a drawer, Aurora pulled a zipper bag out of the box that her mother always kept there. She moved to the refrigerator and filled the bag with ice cubes.

"How was your appointment with the doctor? Does he think he can get you straightened out?"

"Yes. Beau thinks he can get me fixed up and off the pain medications." Now she was going to try ice on the hip he'd adjusted and go with an anti-inflammatory instead of the narcotic-based medicine.

"Beau? Do you mean Dr. Gutterman?" Her mother tossed a small glare over her shoulder and stirred some mysterious spice concoction into the brew. "You shouldn't call him by his first name. It's disrespectful."

"I went to school with Beau. I've known him a long time. I can't call him Dr. Gutterman now. That would be weird."

She tried it out inside her head and it sounded like the name of some old doctor, ready to retire. So *not* the Beau she knew, who was young and vibrant and sexy as hell.

"Well, *I'm* going to call him Dr. Gutterman. It's good to have a hometown boy bringing some business to the area. We need more medical people around here." Sally inspected Aurora through fogged-up glasses and gave her a pointed stare.

Perfect introduction.

"That's good, because he offered me a job." "Offered" was a loose interpretation of their mutual arrangement. *Desperately needed* was more like it.

"What?" The expression on her mother's face looked as if she said she'd just gotten a job at an exotic dance club, not a respectable healthcare business. "You can't be working yet! You're still recovering."

"Mom, it's been over two months since the

accident. When I got out of the rehab facility we agreed I would come here *temporarily*. I can't sit around doing nothing or I'll go mad." She patted her mother on the shoulder. "It'll be all right. It's part-time, and I'm not going to do more than I can handle. That was my agreement with Beau."

That assurance would comfort her mother and buy her some time. Her mother was a controller, and wanted things done her way, which was part of the reason Aurora had left town at such an early age.

"You won't believe this, but his nurse went into labor just after I got there and we delivered the baby together."

"You're kidding!" That got her mother's attention, and she gaped at Aurora. "Everyone's okay?"

"Yes—but that's why he needs a nurse right now, and I start tomorrow."

"Tomorrow? So soon?"

Concern showed in her mother's eyes, and though she hated to disappoint her Aurora knew she had to live her life—not the one her mother had planned for her. Although her mother loved having her around, she had no objective boundaries. It was all or nothing. And Aurora wasn't about to be turned into an invalid lying on the couch while her mother spoon-fed broth into her mouth.

"Yes. Tomorrow. Which brings me to another point. Beau has a small apartment over the office that I'm going to move into."

There—she'd said it. Short. Sweet. Firm. No question about it.

"What? You just *got* here." This time her mother faced her fully, major disappointment on her face. "I had so many plans for us."

"I know you did. But right now what I need is to work, get my career back, and not let the accident take away any more of my life than it already has." She looked into her mother's concerned eyes. "We can still do some of those things you have planned, but I *have* to work. It's what I'm good at, and I need that right now."

Boundaries. It was all about boundaries with her mother.

At that her mother pressed her lips together for a moment as she surveyed her daughter. "You always were too independent."

"For me, there is no such thing, Mom. I'm as independent as I need to be." She shrugged, but remembered Beau's words about taking it easy on her mother. "Everything will be fine. Don't worry."

"I suppose you're going to move tonight, aren't you?"

Pulling away from Aurora, Sally stirred her stew and pouted. Yep, nothing had changed.

"It's best if I move in right away. Most of my things are still in the car or on the porch, so it will be easier this way."

"Easier for whom?" her mother asked, but didn't really require an answer.

"Mom, I'm only going down the road a few miles. We'll still have plenty of time to do things together. I really need to work. You *know* that."

"I guess." She sniffed. "If you can find time to spend with your poor old mother."

Guilt trip. There was always the guilt trip.

"I'll make time—I promise. But first I have to get settled into the apartment and the job. It's not like I'm going back to Virginia right away."

She might never be able to go back to her old life. Perhaps there really *wasn't* a life to go back to there, and she just hadn't realized it.

The car crash seemed to have been a defining moment in her life.

There had been life before the crash. There would be life after the crash. Each of those times was vastly different and she didn't know which way to go. Forward or backward. Or was any direction still forward?

"Well, get your stuff organized and I'll put some of this stew into a container—and some of the bread I made. You can have some home cooking in your new place."

Though her mother didn't like the idea, she appeared to be accepting it. Maybe she was listening to Aurora after all.

"I'd like that. Thank you." Having a bit of home in a new apartment would be a great way to settle in.

"Okay, but I'm going to hold you to it," her mother said, and pointed at her with the wooden spoon, giving a mock glare. "I'm going to find out when the Amish festival is in Smicksburg and we're going."

"That sounds like a great time. I haven't been there in years."

Funny... She'd used to hate driving around to different festivals and displays, museums and other events that had interested her mother, but now she was actually looking forward to it. Late summer and early fall was the time of year for celebrations, harvest gatherings and other festivals in Pennsylvania. There was always something new and interesting to be seen.

But all of it would have to wait until she'd turned her life around.

Two hours later a sharp pain knifed its way through Aurora's hips, but she mustered on and dragged the last of her belongings into the small apartment over the medical clinic.

Beau had arrived with the keys earlier, but had had to rush off to an out-of-hours emergency call. Now, as he returned, he tutted at her.

"Hey, you aren't supposed to be lifting this kind of stuff." Beau took the last box from her, carried it up the stairs and backed through the door. "You'll undo all the adjustments I just did on you."

"I know. I know. I'm sorry." She had to admit that her back was screaming with pain, but she just had to get this done, then she could rest. And ice. Ice was a magical treatment she was just beginning to discover. Thanks to Beau.

"You say that, but you're doing it anyway, right?"

Beau gave her that sideways smile of his. Somehow it chastised and encouraged at the same time.

"You are correct about that. Nurses are terrible patients." She pointed to the plaid couch up against one wall and Beau sat the box on it. "While I had some momentum going I wanted to push through, then it'll be over with, and I can relax."

Without another word Beau placed his hands on her shoulders and turned her to face him. His hands were warm, his touch gentle. Resisting him was impossible and all those unrequited feelings of long ago surfaced as her eyes met his.

What she wouldn't have given to have been in this position ten years ago. Before they'd both been too hurt by life and love. But that was then and this was now. There was no way for them to go back to the innocence they'd once had as kids. Now she was too broken even to try. At least at the moment she felt that way.

"Promise me one thing," he said.

"Okay. What's that?" A deep breath filled her lungs, helped her push away the longings he'd momentarily stirred in her.

"That you'll call me for any heavy stuff you need either to be carried or moved."

"I'll try. I promise." With a nod, she pulled back from him, curiously aroused by his touch and the gentle tones of his voice. Having someone offering to do something nice for her was almost foreign.

Looking back, she could see that her last relationship had been doomed from the get-go, and now she wasn't certain what had really attracted her to the man in the first place. Chad had been a controller, and demanding—which was not the kind of man she wanted in her life. Too much like her father.

But maybe that was what had appealed to her

before she'd realized it. Drawn to the familiar rather than someone new, someone different. Seeing Beau in such contrast made her wonder about her mental state, having put up with that relationship for so long.

"I'm going to hold you to that. Your injuries are overcomeable, but you do need to be babied for a while after every manipulation."

"I see."

She huffed out a breath and changed the subject to one more comfortable to her.

"Speaking of babies—how's Cathy and her baby? Have you talked to her since she got to the hospital?"

"Yes. I just spoke to her a few minutes ago and they're doing great."

The grin that split Beau's face was contagious.

"That's awesome. I still can't believe that happened right in front of us."

"I know—but better here than at home alone or something." Beau opened a box and started to unpack it, then stopped. "Oh, sorry. Do you *want* me to help you?"

"Oh, sure. That's just bedding. You can toss it on the bed. I can make it later."

"No, that's another back-bending chore. I'll help you with it."

Beau shook out the sheets and together they

made up the queen-sized bed that took up the majority of the space in the efficiency apartment.

"Did you tell your mom you were moving out?"

"Yes." Aurora nodded. "It wasn't as bad as I thought it was going to be, but still uncomfortable. I hate confrontation of any sort."

"Yes, but it's necessary sometimes."

"Not according to my mother. If I just went along with all the things she's planned for my life, everything would be just fine." Aurora tossed up one hand for emphasis.

"Except you'd be unhappy."

"Yeah. She kind of forgot about that part."

There was real sympathy in his words, in his expression, and she knew he understood. Had always understood her, even when they were kids.

"She had visions of us being gal pals, or roommates or something."

"Oh. That's kinda weird." Beau's brows crinkled.

Aurora tucked the corner of a sheet in. "Since my dad died last year she's been left without a mission in life, I think."

"How so?"

"Well, she's been a caretaker all her life, and

without Dad needing her all the time she doesn't have enough to keep her occupied."

"Sounds like she needs a project."

Aurora barked out a laugh and it felt good. For the first time in a long time, it felt good. "She does—as long as it isn't me."

The bed was finished in short order, and Aurora's stomach rumbled.

"It's getting to be that time, isn't it?" Beau patted his stomach. "I could eat something myself."

"That's good, because my mom sent along a huge jar of beef stew she made today." Aurora pointed to the jar on the counter. "And homemade bread. If you'd like some I'll be happy to share."

"Awesome. I never turn down free food. Especially homemade." He pulled his phone from his pocket. "Let me check on Chloe first. She's still at the sitter's." After a short conversation, he nodded. "Good to go."

"I'd love to meet her some time."

"Oh, I'm sure you will. I have her in the office sometimes."

"Great. Babies are such fun."

"Says someone who hasn't had a child yet."

"Are you telling me I have a skewed perspective?" With a grin, she parked her hands on her hips.

"Yes."

The grin was returned, and she could see some of the pain of this morning had eased. This banter was fun.

"I dare you to make that statement again after you've been up three nights straight with a teething infant."

"Oh, no, thanks. Not accepting that challenge."

In minutes they had poured the still steaming stew into bowls, buttered bread, and sliced some cheese to go with it.

"Sorry, I don't have any wine. It doesn't go with my medications."

"Oh, that's okay. I'm not much of a drinker."

He scooped some of the stew into his mouth and closed his eyes.

"Oh, my God, that's good. She could open her own restaurant and just serve this. She'd make a fortune." His brows shot up. "Hey, maybe you could talk her into opening her own diner or something? Then she'd be too busy to run your life."

"I like the way you think." Aurora laughed again and relaxed a little more.

Watching him enjoy the stew—a simple meal in her new place—stirred good feelings.

Forbidden feelings—especially after that comment about having her own baby. That had been her lifelong dream, to have a family, but it wasn't meant to be apparently.

Recalling how Beau's wife had tragically died after giving birth reminded her that having a family wasn't without risk. And as she sat there in the small apartment, across from Beau, she wondered if the risks were worth it.

There was only one way to find out.

CHAPTER FOUR

MAYBE COMING HOME *hadn't* been such a bad idea after all. Though returning to her childhood home had been a temporary plan, she liked how it felt right now. Cathy would be off for at least six weeks, so she had that long to think about things and maybe come up with another plan.

"What are you thinking about?" Beau set his spoon down and placed his hand over hers on the table. "You look so intense, so sad."

"I was just thinking how far we've come since high school."

She squeezed his hand and enjoyed the warmth of it in hers. Of course they'd touched. Many times. But now, in the closeness of the little apartment, things seemed different somehow. More grown up. More intimate than she'd imagined.

"You're right." He nodded and kept hold of her hand. "We've come a long way for sure.

Sometimes I look back at who I was then and can't believe I was such a self-centered, immature jerk."

"Oh, Beau!" She leaned back in her chair with a laugh. "You were *not*." No way. At least not the way she remembered it.

"Seriously?" Doubt shone in his eyes. "You don't know half the things I did back then. I thought I was such hot stuff, that I could have any girl I wanted. Cheerleaders. Homecoming queens. Any girl I set my eyes on." He shook his head and drew his mouth to the side. "I was an idiot. All ego. No brains. Not like you."

"I certainly wasn't all brains—and you weren't all ego." Amusement shot through her. "Maybe a little. If you were so bad I could never have been your friend, you know." She lifted one shoulder.

"Really?" Beau's brows shot upward. "How do you figure that, Miss Academic Student of the Year?"

"Oh, that was a silly thing. A fluke, really. I was so shy and introverted in high school I could barely talk to guys, let alone be friends with one." A light pink colored her neck. "Or ever think of going out with a jock."

She leaned closer, conspiratorially.

"I did have a secret crush on you, though. You were totally into the hot babes, and never looked at *me* like that, so I got over it." Or so she'd thought. Until now. Until she'd looked into those green eyes again.

"You... *What*? Now *that's* a surprise." He crossed his arms over his chest and a curious expression showed on his face. His brows came together and an intensity showed in his eyes, as if she'd just told him some deep, dark secret. "You thought I was out of reach, yet you picked me to be friends with? That's odd."

"No, actually..." she said with a laugh, and pointed at him with her spoon. "*You* picked *me*. Don't you remember?"

"No. Refresh my memory."

"In Mrs. Dixon's typing class." A memory and a laugh bubbled up inside her as she recalled him trying to squeeze his bulk behind the small desk the computers had been set on.

"No way. I don't remember that. All I remember is struggling to get my fingers on the keyboard and not totally screw things up."

"Yes—you said if I helped you with typing you'd get me into all the football games the rest of the season for free."

"I did?"

Surprise showed clearly on his face. He didn't remember.

That tidbit disappointed her. He obviously hadn't had the same sort of feelings for her that she'd had for him. This reinforced that she'd been right to keep her feelings to herself. Pining after him would only have brought her heartache.

"Yes, you did."

"I don't remember it that way at all."

"No? Well, that's exactly how it was."

That particular memory was clearly etched in her mind. How embarrassed she'd been when he'd talked to her—then how thrilled she'd been that he'd talked to her! All for naught, as it turned out.

"Nothing is *exactly* anything—let alone memories so old. I think you're yanking my chain." He narrowed his eyes playfully at her, trying to discern the truth.

"You're right, Beau. Nothing is ever exact or perfect, the way we thought it would be when we were kids."

She had to admit that. Nothing in *her* life had been that way. Not ever. And it was one of the reasons she'd left town so soon after nursing school. She'd wanted—*needed*—something in her life to be perfect, and she'd known she'd never get it here. At the time, that was how her mind had worked. Now she wasn't so sure there was a perfect *anything* out there.

At the time she'd thought her happiness had lain out there. Somewhere. Somewhere else.

Somewhere new, different, exotic. Someplace where she knew she'd fit in. Where no one knew her past or had preconceived notions of what she should be. No one would try to make her fit into a mold they'd developed for her. Where she could live and be herself, with no one to please *except* herself.

Beau leaned back and patted his abdomen again. "Nothing's perfect except for this stew. *I'd* be tempted to stay with your mother just for her cooking."

With his words the tension in her eased and she relaxed.

"I know. She *is* a great cook, but it doesn't come without strings."

Yet another reason she'd had to leave her mother's home as soon as she could. But despite all her faults Aurora loved her mother, and had to accept her as she was—not continue to wish she were different. Another part of her childhood that she had to let go of.

"That's too bad, 'cause she's a really great cook."

One corner of Aurora's mouth lifted. "And then there's her bread." Another thing Aurora had to admit was a huge bonus of hanging out with her mother. She loved to bake and was excellent at it. "She tried to teach me, but I only made lead bread so I gave up."

"It's amazing."

"Incredible."

"Which is unfortunate."

"Why?" A confused frown crossed Aurora's face.

"Well, if she was a good cook and a bad baker, then I could justify a strike against her. If she was bad at both, that would be two strikes."

"I see. So since she's good at both, then it's two points in her favor?"

Fortunately, Beau hadn't lost his sense of humor. It had kept him from going crazy with grief after his wife's death. It made him see things a little differently, but he liked it that way. It had helped him turn himself around after the worst time in his life. It had helped him begin to view life in a different way.

"You got it. You catch on quick."

He winked, and a little squiggle of pleasure shot through him as she held his gaze just a little bit longer. That was interesting. She'd had a crush on him and he'd never noticed? He was an idiot. At least he had been back then. Now he could appreciate what a great woman Aurora had become.

"You have a strange scoring system." She laughed and shook her head.

The outer corners of her eyes crinkled up and

the laugh came from her chest, not her throat, and was a genuine expression. That made him feel good. That he'd made her laugh when the past few months had been filled with anything but joy for either of them.

"Well, it works for me. I have to say that."

After they'd finished, he took the dishes to the sink. Aurora rose with obvious stiffness in her back.

"Just put them in the sink. I'll deal with them later."

Beau could hear the fatigue in her voice, and her eyes were dark with pain. "Come here."

She approached, and he turned her to face away from him, her back against his chest.

"What? What are you doing?"

"Just relax. I'm going to do another gentle treatment on you. A fine tuning."

"Er...*now*?" Surprise lifted her voice into a question.

"Yes, now." He pushed her long hair off her shoulder and to the front. "Cross your arms over your chest. I'm going to hug you from behind."

"How is a backward hug going to help?"

"Shh. Trust me. Take a breath and relax."

Although she performed the movements as he'd directed, when she lifted her arms and put them on top of his, and he embraced her from behind, something in him changed.

He struggled to tamp down the attraction he felt for her in that moment. She'd been there in his formative years and he trusted her. He had always trusted her. Now he needed to be strong for her—not some affection-starved, struggling single father who needed feminine companionship.

Getting a grip on his hormones, he secured her against his chest, wishing for just a second or two that things could be different between them. They'd been friends. They'd always be friends. He wouldn't change that for a quick escape between the sheets. Aurora was more important to him than that. Way more.

"Now, just relax. Lean back against me and let me hold your weight."

"I don't know if I can. I'm so tense."

Her chest rose and fell quickly with her breathing. With one hand he eased her head back to rest against his left shoulder.

"Close your eyes and listen to my voice. Take a breath in. Let it out slowly."

Beau rocked her gently back and forth while he tuned in to the feel of her body against his, waiting for the moment she relaxed. Her head nestled perfectly against his shoulder and felt so very right. The way her back and hips lined up against his chest was an exact fit.

All she had to do was turn her face toward

him and it would be in the perfect position for him to place his lips against hers, to breathe in her scent and take this embrace to a whole new level. He hadn't held a woman in a long time and now, holding Aurora this way, he realized how much he'd missed having a woman in his life.

How much he missed Julie.

Choking down the emotions swirling in him, he swallowed hard. Distracting himself right now was as important as distracting her.

Eventually she relaxed her head against his shoulder and the tension in her back eased.

The moment he felt it shift he lifted her by the arms and gave her a quick shake.

"Oh!" She cried out at the sudden jerking movement, but he hadn't hurt her—just surprised her. "Oh, wow. I feel different already."

"Don't tense up. Just stay with me. Rock with me."

He set her feet on the floor, but didn't release her. He kept her snuggled against his chest, taking a second or two to savor the feel of her body against his even if it was wrong.

"It's hard not to brace myself. I've been so locked up for months that feeling the release, the relief, is kind of strange at the moment."

One of her hands patted his arm as he held her. The gentle motion of her touch on his skin stirred him and he had to tamp down his reaction again.

"I know. You'll have to get used to feeling good again and then *that* will be your norm."

Slowly, reluctantly, he released her, and she took a moment to turn inward and check her body. He could see that she liked the feeling of relief.

"Like I said, soon you'll be swinging from the rafters in your dad's barn."

"Beau…" She reached one hand out and put it on his chest. The light in her eyes, the beauty of her, was almost irresistible.

"You're welcome."

He swallowed hard, trying to resist the attraction that had swooped down to surprise him. After the wonderful relationship he'd had with Julie he'd not expected to be attracted to another woman. At least not so soon. Shaking himself mentally, he berated himself for going down that path. Now wasn't the time. A year hadn't passed yet and he was still mourning Julie, still in love with her—wasn't he? Or had the time come for him to move on?

"I don't know how to thank you for helping me."

"Every day it's going to get better and better."

Irritated with himself, he moved away before he was tempted to cup his hands around her face and draw her closer, to kiss those full ruby lips and breathe in her scent. Aurora was his friend, and now his employee. This wasn't the time to take his libido out for a stroll.

"You can pay me back by helping me get the office going and organized."

That was the goal. That was what he needed to be focused on—not on having thoughts about Aurora that would only get him into trouble.

"Oh, for sure."

When Beau released her she was amazed. Not only could she stand up straight for the first time in ages, but the pain was almost gone. And she had Beau to thank for it.

"Thank you so much."

Cupping her hands under his arms and hugging him to her, she pressed her chest against his. He was strong, and muscled, and not as lean as he'd been in high school—but, then again, neither of them were. When his arms encircled her she had that feeling she'd always been looking for—that feeling of coming home, of belonging, of being needed and wanted, of being able to lean on someone.

She abruptly pulled back. That was *not* the direction her thoughts should be taking her.

Although it had been just a flash of emotion, the feeling was powerful, and she had to pull back before she did something she'd regret. Her future wasn't here in Brush Valley. She wasn't going to be in Pennsylvania for long. Just a few more weeks. Maybe a month or two, tops. Indulging in an affair with an old friend just wasn't going to benefit either of them. Their lives were entangled, but only as friends, and she didn't want to destroy that by giving in to a momentary flash of physical need.

They weren't children any longer. She had a grown woman's needs and desires. A man like Beau would certainly have his own needs, too. Opening *that* pandora's box with him would be something she could never take back. She would never be able to shut the lid on those old feelings if she let them out. Back then they'd been just kids, trying to figure out who they were. Now they were different. Grown up. The consequences were much greater—especially now that he had a child. Hurting him or being hurt wasn't something she wanted. He was still in recovery after the loss of his wife, and losing their friendship would only end in more loss for them both.

"You're welcome."

When she looked up at him the look in his eyes was curious, as if he'd felt something too and didn't know what to say about it. Then he looked away, cleared his throat, and the moment was gone. She breathed a sigh of relief. This was *not* the time to crack the lid on that box.

"So, tomorrow I'll start on that messy desk of yours and get it organized."

Distraction. Lots and lots of distraction. That was the key to keeping those feelings of hers subdued.

"That will be great."

An alert beeped on his phone.

"Oh, that'll be Ginny. Chloe must be ready to go home." He double-checked the message and nodded. "See you in the morning, then?"

"You got it."

As he turned she wanted to say something, say anything, but she didn't know quite how to put it into words.

"Beau?"

"Yeah?"

He paused and looked at her. Really looked at her. As if he saw her, saw *into* her, knew what she was going to say even before the words formed in her mind. Her last boyfriend had always seemed like he was looking through her, was looking for the next woman to capture his attention. But not Beau, not now. Not in this moment.

"I... I just remembered something my mother mentioned. Brush Valley Day is coming in a few weeks."

At the last second she changed her mind, not wanting to say anything that would interfere in her new job, or the dynamic of their friendship. That had to come first. No matter what.

"I remember seeing that somewhere. You'd like that day off? No problem."

"No. I mean, yes. What I'm trying to get to is that it might be an opportunity to do some community outreach—set up a blood pressure clinic, give flu shots, stuff like that."

She hoped he'd like the idea. Even though it was off the top of her head, it was pretty good.

"You're brilliant—do you know that?" He took three steps toward her, clutched her by the shoulders and planted a hard kiss on her cheek. "That's a perfect idea, and I never even thought about it."

"Fall is festival time. Might as well take advantage of it when it's in our backyard, right?" The heat of a blush bubbled up inside her— pride at having an idea that hadn't immediately been shot down by someone who thought it was stupid or outrageous. "I think it could work nicely."

"Absolutely. We can have a sign-up sheet that will offer follow-up appointments and get people in to see the office. Really show off what we offer here."

Excitement glowed in his eyes.

"We can hand out fliers or appointment cards for people to take home with them—or magnets for their refrigerators with first aid information on them."

The energy pulsing around him was contagious.

"Are you sure you're a nurse? 'Cause those sound like excellent marketing ideas." Beau shook his head and looked at her in admiration.

"I do like marketing. Not like for used cars, though. Just finding ways to get services to people who need them."

"Well, you're hired."

"I think you already did that."

"Right."

He snapped his fingers and pointed at her with a grin. The joy that had been bubbling in her system now gushed over.

"Tomorrow at lunch we'll order something in and make a plan. Write up your ideas tonight, and we'll go from there."

"Great. See you in the morning."

He walked over to the door and Aurora followed him.

When he turned back, he paused with his hand on the doorknob. "It's great to see you again, and I can't tell you how happy I am to be working with you."

"Me too, Beau. Me too."

"Goodnight."

As Aurora closed the door she listened as his footsteps echoed down the wooden stairs. A grin split her face, and she felt like she'd just walked a date to the door.

"Oh, dear. I may be in serious trouble."

CHAPTER FIVE

BEAU PICKED UP Chloe and drove home, but his thoughts were still in that apartment over his office. Aurora had really gotten him thinking about so many things—like how to promote his office, his services, how he could be a better and long-term part of the community.

Things he'd never thought about before. Things he probably shouldn't be thinking about now. Like how good it had felt to hold her in his arms, to laugh with her, to feel whole and human again after losing his wife.

He'd been in survival mode after Julie's death. Learning how to raise a baby alone as well as opening a business had taken up all of his available brain cells. Those had been dark, dark days, but now he was able to see the possibilities for his future as a father, as a doctor. Maybe someday as a partner in a relationship again.

He glanced in the rearview mirror at his

sleeping daughter. "She's right, baby girl. We have to be part of the community—not just live here like we don't belong in it."

That meant changes were on the way. Big changes. And he was finally ready for them. At least in the office and his business life. His personal life was still something that was going to get left behind for a while. Looking at the curly-haired replica of Julie sitting in the back seat, he felt his chest burn, emotion pulsing.

Was he ready to open himself up to anything outside of the little world he'd built with just him and Chloe? Could he ever have another relationship like he'd had with Julie? Was he even ready to consider dipping into the dating pool again? With a child, it was so much harder, with so many more things to consider.

He sighed, not knowing the answer to any of those questions. He wasn't sure he was ready, but then again, was anyone ever totally sure they were ready? For anything?

A noise from the baby in the back drew his attention. Didn't Chloe deserve to have a mother in her life? Not just a daddy who ran in too many directions? This little angel, the love of his life, deserved everything, and it was up to him to provide it. Somehow.

The empty house offered no warm greeting, no glowing lights to let him know someone was there waiting for him. He gathered Chloe and headed into the quiet, solemn house as a cloud of heaviness lay over his shoulders and pressed down on him. He hung his backpack on a peg beside the door, placed Chloe in her basinet, and opened the fridge out of habit, even though he'd already eaten with Aurora.

He noticed the meager supplies inside. Hadn't he started a list of groceries? He'd so not appreciated how well Julie had kept their life organized until he'd had to do it all himself.

This wasn't the life he'd imagined for himself just a few years ago. Not at all.

He'd expected to come home to his happy wife and snuggly baby, for them to go on outings together, to get bundled up and play in the snow, to have picnics at the lake and relax in the shade of a willow tree. That had been his dream, what he'd envisioned having with Julie, but it had all come crashing down around his shoulders late in her pregnancy, when she'd collapsed in his arms.

Beau sighed, not wanting to go back and visit that horrible memory tonight. Tonight all he wanted to do was relax and put his feet up, but his emotions, his memories, had other plans.

He grabbed a beer and twisted the top off, but there was laundry and dishes to do, and the dog needed to be let out for a run.

Fortunately his property sat on five acres of mostly wooded land, and Daisy could take a run without the neighbors being bothered by her roaming. He never feared that she wouldn't come back. She was the other constant in his life. The loyalty of this wonderful animal had gotten him through some terrible days. Knowing she needed him too, mattered.

After a futile hour of household chores and dealing with a fussy infant Beau tried to feed Chloe what she normally ate. But tonight nothing was working. The little miss was *not* happy.

Maybe she was teething. Maybe she had an upset stomach. Maybe she needed something he hadn't even thought of.

Babies were generally pretty easy to diagnose. Food. Sleep. Diapers. After those were checked off, then it was anyone's guess. Perhaps tonight she was missing her mother the way he was. Could she even have a memory of her mother?

The heat and weight of Daisy's head resting on his leg attracted his attention.

"What can I do for you, girl?"

He spoke gently to the chocolate Labrador who had seen him through the thick and thin of the last year. She adjusted her head to a more comfortable position and cast golden eyes filled with adoring patience and eternal understanding up at him. She didn't give him any real answers, but an idea did come to him as he stared at her.

"Let's go for a ride. Maybe Chloe will fall asleep in the car."

At the mention of the word *car* and the jangle of keys Daisy whipped her tail around in eager anticipation. She even drooled on his leg. Obviously she needed more attention than he was giving her, too.

"Come on, girl. Let's get out of here for a while."

Within minutes he'd gathered his daughter and stowed her in her car seat. Daisy, a wagging mess of excitement, stood on the other side of the back seat, sticking her head out the window, sniffing the early evening air to her heart's content.

They drove for an hour, until the sun sank below the horizon. Beau didn't know where he was going, but on these narrow highways and back roads he didn't care. He could drive all over this township and never get lost. He'd delivered newspapers as a kid on his bike, then in a beat-up SUV. He knew every rutted lane and pothole-filled road.

Memories of those easy days filled him with nostalgia, and some of the tension in his shoulders eased. Now that Aurora was back a little bit more of his life was complete. He'd missed her and their friendship. Their lives had gone in different directions after school, but she'd been the kind of friend he'd been able to count on when he'd needed one—and, man, did he need one now.

Absentmindedly, he drove past the clinic on his way back home. It was just force of habit, he told himself, to check on his business one last time before the end of the day and make sure nothing was amiss, that he'd locked everything up tight. It wasn't an excuse to see Aurora again.

As he slowed the vehicle, tires crunching in the gravel parking lot, he looked at the apartment window overhead. A dim light glowed behind the curtains.

Was Aurora still up? Was she reading before bed the way he knew she always had? In high school she'd always had a book in her hand, so it wouldn't surprise him if she was reading one now.

So many feelings swirled around in him, confused him. He didn't know what to do. Looking in the rearview mirror at Chloe's sleeping face, he blew out a sigh of relief. *Finally.*

Having such a tiny person depend on him so completely was something he was still getting used to. Though she was only nine months old, she was changing every day. Some new issue, new problem or new growth-related thing he had to learn about raising a baby came up constantly. Although he was a physician, trained in pediatrics, being a father brought a completely different perspective. When it was your own kid that was sick, or hurt, or troubled, the game changed.

His phone rang and he jumped, then answered it even though it was an unfamiliar out-of-state number. "Dr. Gutterman."

"What are you doing out there?"

Aurora's soft voice posed the question, and he grinned, then looked up through the windshield as she looked down at him.

"I'm not stalking you, if that's what you think." He waved.

"Well, why not?" She waved back.

That made him laugh. She'd always made him laugh, and it felt good inside his chest now. Some of the heaviness that had been following him tonight lifted. After months of grieving over the unexpected death of his wife, this lighthearted feeling was foreign, but he welcomed it. Needed it.

"I guess I could start...since I know where you live."

"And work. Don't forget that."

"I won't."

Having her beside him in the office was going to be so amazing.

"Seriously, what are you doing down there?"

Looking up at the window, Beau could see her there, with the curtain pulled back. She looked like a widow of old, standing in her window watching for her man to return from the sea. But he was no sailor, she was no widow, and there was no sea.

"I took Chloe for a drive because she was so fussy. We ended up here to check on the building, because I didn't remember locking up, and I didn't know where to go from here."

"Don't you want to go home yet?"

He paused. Was he that transparent? Then he sighed. "No. Not really. So here we are."

"Why don't you bring her up? We can fix a bed for her here and see if she'll rest."

"It's late. I don't want to bother you."

Though he said the right words, to give her a way out, he didn't really want to go home. It wasn't home any longer—just a place he lived. He wanted her company. Was it wrong?

"It's not that late, and if I didn't want to do it I wouldn't offer."

"I have a dog, too." He cringed.

Her soft laugh flitted into his ear and the tightness in his chest eased some more. "Well, bring the whole family and we'll be just fine."

"You're awesome."

Carefully he collected Chloe, who still slept

and cuddled against his shoulder, then let Daisy out. When he turned toward the outside staircase Aurora stood there, bathed in the light from the kitchen. Surrounded by a golden halo, she looked like an angel. Maybe right now she was.

He didn't know how he was going to repay this woman for her kindness, her generosity and her friendship, but somehow he was going to. Giving her a job and an apartment wasn't enough.

"So, this is Chloe?" Aurora kept her voice to a whisper.

"This is my baby girl."

Beau turned around to give Aurora a look at her beautiful face. As she was only nine months old she hadn't evolved her own looks, but he thought she looked like Julie.

"Put her on the bed. See if she'll settle down and sleep there." On the way past, she reached out and patted the little girl on the back. "She's beautiful, Beau. Just beautiful."

"Looks like her mother, fortunately. I think so, anyway. My mother says she looks like me. Isn't that what mothers always say?"

"Babies tend to favor their fathers in the first six months."

"Really? I wonder why that is?" That made him frown. He hadn't heard that before.

"Probably some evolutionary thing that helps

fathers bond with their children." She shrugged, and pulled the covers back on the bed.

He placed Chloe face down, away from the pillows, covered her with her blanket and tucked in the little ratty stuffed dog she loved.

"God, I hope she sleeps." He rubbed his face with his hands and stifled a yawn. "I'm so tired I could sleep standing up."

"Why don't you forget about everything on your shoulders right now and lie down? The bed's big enough for the three of us, I think."

Beau's eyes popped wide in surprise. "I hadn't planned on staying the night. I don't want to inconvenience you on your first night here."

"Look. It's not quite ten o'clock. I usually read for a while." Aurora glanced down at the sleeping child. "We're all wiped out. Let's just call it a night, okay?"

"Frankly, Aurora, I'm too tired to try to convince you otherwise." He removed his boots and stretched out on the bed beside his sleeping daughter. "I don't know how to thank you."

He closed his eyes, sighed, and flung an arm over his face. The peace that he needed, that he sought every night at his empty house, was here in this little apartment. It immediately surrounded him, flinging off the dead weight of grief clinging to his shoulders and bringing relief he'd not known possible.

"Just get some sleep. That's all the thanks I need."

"Thank you."

Morning brought a streak of sun shining through the window onto Beau's face. He lay on his side, facing the wall, and blinked as his memory failed to alert him to his immediate surroundings. They looked familiar, but strange at the same time.

Night had dropped on him like a brick building going down, and he'd slept like the dead for a change. Taking a deep breath in and looking around, he saw the boxes he'd carried in for Aurora last night, still sitting where he'd left them, and realized he'd fallen asleep at her place.

That was why it looked and seemed so familiar. He'd lived here for a few weeks with Chloe after Julie's death, while he got his office space converted from ready for animals to ready for people. That way he'd had a place to stay, it was nearby, and it had allowed him to grieve for Julie without being confronted by her clothing in their closet, her make-up in their bathroom, or the lingering fragrance of her perfume in the air. Facing the truth of her absence in their home was more than he'd been able to bear at the time.

He sat and looked over his shoulder. Pressure filled his chest at the sight.

Chloe slept like an angel, cuddled up against Aurora's chest, and Aurora's hand rested protectively on her back. Even in sleep they were both angels, for entirely different reasons. One had saved his soul, and the other was going to save his business.

Some of his movements must have awakened Aurora because she took a breath and stirred. Her baby blues fluttered open, and she looked over at him with a sexy sleepiness he'd never imagined seeing in her eyes. At that moment he could just imagine waking up with her in his arms, taking his time to rouse her with kisses and caresses, sharing the morning with skin against skin.

When she looked into his eyes, still half asleep, and smiled, he realized his body was trying to take him down a road he didn't want to go. At least not yet. He needed a shower. A cold one. *Fast*.

"Morning," he whispered, and turned away. He didn't need to see any more of Aurora if he was going to get through this morning without embarrassing himself.

"Good morning." Aurora stirred again and rose, extricating herself from Chloe without disturbing her.

"Looks like you've done that before," he said, impressed with skills it had taken him many months to acquire. Being a dad, learning everything he'd had to learn, had not been easy. At least not to him. Women, though, seemed to have some instinct about it. Probably why the human race had survived.

"Lots of practice."

"Really? How?"

"Babysitting as a teenager, then being a pediatric nurse. I've had lots of practice getting babies to go to sleep and stay that way."

"When she was a newborn I spent *hours* trying to get her to sleep for fifteen minutes. Maybe you can teach me a few of those tricks as I obviously still need them."

He shook his head and pushed his hair out of his face, thinking again that he either needed to get a haircut or start wearing a man bun. *Not happening.*

"Happy to."

She stretched and pulled an extra-long sweatshirt over her head, which covered her from her neck to mid-thigh, and stuck her feet into fuzzy black slippers. Though it wasn't the lingerie of a fashion model, the look was certainly endearing and totally Aurora.

A rhythmic slapping on the floor caught his

attention and he saw Daisy by the door, looking up at him with a message in her eyes.

"Time to go out, girl?" The slapping got faster and she sat up, eagerness written all over her face, if that were possible. "Okay. Let's go."

He turned to Aurora.

"I'm going to take her out, then I'll be back."

"Okay." She glanced at the sleeping infant, sucking on her lip. "She'll be fine."

With a nod, Beau opened the door and the dog rushed out, bounced down the stairs, then raced over to a patch of grass and squatted.

"Good girl."

For a few minutes he took her out to the fenced pasture that had been used to hold livestock at the veterinary practice. What Beau liked about the location of the clinic was that it was surrounded by green fields and acres of forest after that—not parking lots and rows of buildings. City living was not for him. Not after going to college there and then working at a clinic. This was home. Country living would always be home for him.

No other business could build too close, and there was plenty of parking, plenty of room for growth. There was even enough room to build a house back by the edge of the woods, so he could combine his business and his home in one property.

Thoughts of the house he'd shared with his wife brought no joy, no sense of peace or of belonging. Now, it was just a place to put his belongings, not a place to which he had much attachment. When the business got going he was definitely going to put a house at the edge of the woods and sell the other house.

Daisy returned shortly, after a romp around the grass, wet with morning dew. "Find any rabbits, girl?" At the mention of rabbits, her ears perked up. "We'd better go back inside, before you find something you really want to chase."

They reentered the apartment to the smell of coffee brewing and something mysterious sizzling on the stove.

"Hope you're hungry."

"I wasn't hungry until I smelled that." He leaned closer to the sizzling skillet and inhaled. "Oh, *my*. What is it? It smells heavenly."

Aurora gave him a smile and stirred. "In my family, we call it *stuff*."

"Why? Doesn't it deserve a better name than that?"

"Well, there's all kinds of *stuff* in it. I guess it was easier." She shrugged and continued to stir. "My grandmother made it, and it was passed down from someone else in the family before her. We used to make it before family events, or when the guys would go hunting, things like that."

A soft look covered her face as she stirred the ingredients in the skillet.

"What are you thinking right now?"

There had been an unguarded moment when she'd talked of her family. Though there had been some trouble with her and her family, he knew she loved her parents.

"Oh, it's nothing. It's just…" She shrugged and gave a head-tilt. "It just reminds me of good times when I was growing up. Cousins. Holidays." She gave him a glance, then returned to stirring. "The age of innocence, you know? The days before you knew what life was really like."

"Life can suck sometimes. But other times…" A lump formed in his throat as he looked at the baby on the bed. "It's more precious than you could ever imagine."

She met his gaze then, looking deep into him, trying to see if he'd told her the truth. It was the truth as much as he knew.

Stepping closer, he took one of her hands in his and gave it a squeeze. "Somehow, deep down, there is hope and joy that pushes away the pain and sorrow. We have to wait sometimes for that to happen. The older I get, the more I realize that timing is everything."

He'd seen it. He knew it. He just had to hold

on to it through the tough times. Maybe that time for him—for them—was now. Together.

"Sometimes we wait a long time to be in the right place at the right time to get what we want...what we need."

Aurora gave him a watery smile and held his gaze. "I hope you're right, Beau."

"I know I am." He placed his hand on her shoulder for a quick squeeze. "I also know I'm ready for some of that *stuff*." He patted his stomach, which had begun to gnaw a hole in his abdomen. "Is it ready yet? I'm starved."

Aurora laughed, and sniffed back that hint of tears he'd seen in her eyes and heard in her voice.

"Okay. Stuff coming right up."

In just a minute she'd dished up a plate full of it, set it and a cup of coffee in front of him—and he'd never been happier with a simple meal, in a tiny apartment, early on a late summer morning.

After the first bite, he closed his eyes. "Oh, my God. This is fabulous. It definitely needs a better name."

A pleased smile appeared on her face and in her eyes. As he watched she even seemed to stand a little taller, too.

"Is your pain any better this morning?"

Her eyes popped wide. "Oh, wow. I almost

forgot about it!" She leaned to the left, then to the right. "I can't believe that."

"You don't have to put yourself *in* pain to realize you've been *out* of pain, you know." He'd seen many patients do that.

"I didn't realize I was doing that."

She moved her back to the left and right a little more, then laughed in pure joy and it was good to hear.

"I want to dance now." She did a little wobbly pirouette, then grabbed onto the counter for stability. "Whoa. I'm a bad ballet dancer, but this is so awesome, Beau." She grabbed hold of his forearm. "*Awesome!* This is the first night I've slept without pain in months. *Months!* You have no idea how fantastic this is."

"No, I don't—but I like how fantastic it looks on you." Had he just said that out loud? "I mean, it's great that you're feeling so good and it shows."

Clearing his throat, he hoped she hadn't heard that.

"I don't suppose this will last, will it?"

The vulnerability, the fear and need in her eyes as she stood so close to him, was about all it was going to take for him to pull her into his arms and kiss her. Those boundaries they'd had as kids were gone. He was a man fully grown, and she was no longer the off-limits virgin on a pedestal he'd thought her to be back then. She was beautiful, and ripe, and he wanted her.

Heat and lust, experience and desire pulsed between them. He felt it. So did she.

Focusing on the moment, he pushed away those other thoughts that would only lead to trouble for both of them. "It *will* last, Aurora. As long as you continue to strengthen, and stretch, and do the work you need to do, it will last. The work will be life-long, though."

"Well..." She looked away again and took a step back from him, reached for her coffee with a trembling hand. "It's like any new habit or new thing you do, right? You have to work at it until it's second nature."

"Right."

He was glad she'd moved back. Each of them was vulnerable in different ways, and to put those two together would be a powder keg of heat and sex he didn't think either of them was ready for just yet.

"You'll be fine." He glanced at Chloe, who still slept, one finger in her mouth. "If you don't mind, I'm going to go downstairs and shower while she's asleep. I've got spare clothes in the car, so I'll grab those."

"No problem. But what about Daisy? She needs some food, too."

At the mention of her name, that long tail of hers began to thump on the floor.

"Right. Well, I guess I'll pack up the whole gang and—"

"No—wait. What I'm trying to say is...why don't you go home and shower, change, and bring back Daisy's food? She can stay here, then be with us at the clinic so she's not lonely at home all by herself."

"Bring her to the clinic? Seriously?"

But other healthcare businesses had mascots or resident animals, and Daisy was as well-behaved as any of them...

"Why didn't I think of that?" He looked down at his beloved canine. "She's certainly got the temperament for it."

"Go. I'll hang out with the gang while you go have a peaceful shower for once."

"Aurora, you've no idea what you've done."

The relief that flooded through him was monumental. He hadn't had a moment of peace—not really—since Chloe was born. There had been so much to do and not enough time to do it. Things like leisurely showers had been cut to the bone.

"What?" Her eyes widened with worry. "What did I do?"

"You're about to make yourself indispensable to me." He was not kidding.

"I'm sorry. I'm not meaning to. If that's a problem I can stop, and you can do it all yourself."

Though the words were not what he wanted to hear, he could see the teasing light in her eyes and the grin about to burst across her face.

"No. No, thank you." That humor of hers was infectious. "I'll take indispensable any time."

With a last glance at Chloe, he headed out the door, with a lightness to his footsteps and in his heart that had been absent just yesterday.

In an hour he was back and ready to go. Daisy was fed and walked again. Chloe ate some of the "stuff" that Aurora had made, and he was about to take her to Ginny's house for the day.

For the first time in a long while all was right in his world.

CHAPTER SIX

WHEN BEAU LEFT with Daisy, to take Chloe to the sitter, Aurora took a deep breath and blew it out, trying to blow away the feelings swirling inside her. Having company on her first night in the new place had been good, but it had made her think of things best left alone. Surges of her teenage dreams, of having a family of her own, had emerged. Thoughts of being married, having her own children. Things she thought she'd put away long ago.

She was certain her mind was playing tricks on her, and she *hadn't* seen that flash of interest in Beau's eyes—that he *hadn't* been drawing closer to her more than once.

Perhaps it was because she'd been stuck in the rehab center for two months and she was lonely, or needed to reconnect with her friends. There were so many other reasons why she'd begun to think of Beau in a way she hadn't for a long, long time. Not simply that he'd wanted her. Confidence in her womanhood, her sexuality, had been destroyed by her ex. Beau was the first man to look at her like he was interested, like he found her attractive, and that was heady stuff. Her ego stood a little straighter.

Be that as it may, at the moment she could barely take care of herself, so she needed to cut it out right now. Focus only on why she was here in Brush Valley, on the fact that she was only here *temporarily*.

Everything about her life was temporary.

Everything about Beau's life was permanent.

Having some sort of unfulfillable fantasy about a man and a baby being plopped down into the middle of her life and rescuing her from herself was just ludicrous.

She'd worked hard to get out of Pennsylvania, to make a life for herself elsewhere. Letting a few weeks and some idealistic fantasy about her and Beau ruin all of that wasn't going to happen. This was not her life.

She took a few breaths and blew them out. Again.

When she arrived at the clinic she realized she didn't have a key to get in, but knew Beau would be back shortly.

"Add that to the list of things I need to do. Get a key to the clinic."

Pushing aside those fanciful thoughts of having a relationship with Beau, she focused on the here and now.

A car arrived with two people in it, and Beau pulled in right behind them, with Daisy hanging out the back window. She barked once when she saw Aurora, which made her laugh, and the tone of her heart changed in an instant. Life was good right now, and Aurora relaxed. The day was beautiful, with the sun warm and shining, a light breeze lifted her hair and teased her cheek. Even though this time was temporary, there was no reason she couldn't enjoy it.

Beau let Daisy out of the SUV and looked at her with a grin lighting up his face. "It's a good day when people are waiting at the door to get in."

"It is." Aurora had to agree with that. "I think I should have a key, in case you're late or something—don't you?"

"Absolutely." He led the way with Daisy to the clinic door and opened it. "Come on in, folks. Give us a few minutes to get organized, then we'll see you right away."

"It's okay. You go ahead. It'll probably take me that long just to get in the door." The woman getting out of the car waved them ahead as her caregiver retrieved a walking frame.

Within a few minutes Beau had opened the doors, turned on the lights and grabbed Daisy's bed from the car. She followed him, sniffed it, then turned around in a circle three times and settled into a tight ball beside Aurora at the desk.

"Sign in, please, and we'll get you back to see the doctor shortly."

"It's okay, dear. Take your time. I'm in no hurry." The elder woman walked stiffly with her walker, and the young caregiver in attendance. "We'll wait over here."

"Thank you… Mrs. Kinsey." Aurora read the name, then looked at the woman, trying to place her. "Mrs. *Janet* Kinsey?"

The woman didn't stop, but nodded. "Yep. That's me."

"You were the high school librarian, weren't you?"

"For forty-five years." She negotiated her way to the chair and turned around to peer at Aurora through thick glasses.

"I graduated there a few years ago. I'm Aurora Hunt."

"I remember you now. Always a bright smile, if I remember correctly."

At that, Aurora couldn't help but grin. Another fond memory was bubbling up inside her. All the wonderful times she'd spent in the library, feeding her reading addiction. "That's what you remember about me?"

"Was I wrong?" Mrs. Kinsey turned to her attendant. "It's that smile I've never forgotten."

"Me either, Mrs. Kinsey."

Beau appeared at the desk and surprised Aurora. Though he spoke to the elderly woman, his gaze was on her.

"That smile is etched in *my* memory, too."

With that, he stepped over to the woman and offered his assistance.

"Let's get you back and have a look at you."

"Oh, thank you, Beau."

She abandoned her walker for the arm of a strong, handsome man. Nothing wrong with her decision-making processes.

"You're a dear, too." She patted his arm and held on to him.

Aurora took her vital signs. "Your blood pressure is up, Mrs. Kinsey. Are you taking your medication?" She referred to the patient's medication list on the computer chart.

"Yes, but I ran out on Saturday and didn't realize 'til then."

"We'll get you squared away." Aurora put the equipment down.

"I know it's none of my business, but I was wondering...are you and Beau dating?"

"Dating? Oh, no. His nurse went on maternity leave yesterday. We're just friends and co-workers. I'm helping him get the clinic organized."

The older woman snorted, and cast a look of disbelief at her caregiver. "That's what Mr. Kinsey and I said when we were working together and people asked. *Just friends*." She slapped her thigh and barked out a laugh. "'Til I got pregnant—then it was all over, with a quick wedding at the JP."

"Oh, really. There's nothing like that going on between us, Mrs. Kinsey."

The heat of a blush worked its way up Aurora's neck. That was always a dead giveaway when she was emotional. Just because she'd had carnal thoughts about Beau it didn't make them true, so technically she wasn't lying.

"Guess we'll see how true that is if I see an announcement in the paper someday."

"An announcement about what? Tuning in to the gossip of the day, are you?"

Beau smiled and gave his best doctor face to his patient.

"Oh, I'm just giving Aurora a hard time."

"I'm going to head out to the front. I think I heard someone." Aurora made a beeline for the door.

"Awfully flighty for a nurse, don't you think?" Mrs. Kinsey asked Beau.

"She's just fine. Today's her first day, so I think we'll have to give her a break."

"She's a fine girl. Make someone a good wife,

too." The woman gave him a pointed look over her glasses.

"You seem to be pretty focused on getting one or both of us hitched."

"Yes, well…" She sniffed and looked away for a second. "I'm itching for some grandchildren, but my kids aren't cooperating, so I guess I'm taking my frustration out on anyone I can." She patted Beau on the arm. "Sorry about that."

"I'm certain you're right about Aurora. I just hope she doesn't leave me to go on maternity leave the way my last nurse did."

"You need yourself a good woman, Beau. It's been enough time now. You'll never forget Julie, but moving forward is important, and that little baby of yours needs a mama." She patted his hand, offering sympathy in a simple gesture.

"Thank you, Mrs. Kinsey. I appreciate your concern. But how about we talk about *you* today?"

How was he going to steer the conversation away from this direction?

"I don't think talking about me and Aurora will get your blood pressure back where it belongs."

"You can divert the conversation, but the facts remain the same." With that, she huffed out a sigh of resignation.

"No doubt. Now, what's bothering you today?"

Though Beau didn't let on to his patient that she'd struck a nerve with him, he was irritated that people thought they could tell him what he needed to do with his life. That was the one giant problem with living in a small town. Everybody knew everybody's business, and if they didn't they thought they should. Right now all he needed to do was get his clinic to the next level and take care of his daughter and his dog. That was all. Not have his intriguing thoughts about Aurora reinforced.

He listened to her chatter on about this and that, general aches and pains, all attributed to the aging process of a seventy-year-old and maybe a bad pair of shoes.

"Give me that bag of dirt," she said to her caregiver, who handed her a zipper bag of a white powdery substance, which she held out in front of Beau.

"What's that?" It looked like powdered sugar—or an illicit substance he didn't want to know about.

"Diatomaceous earth. Ever heard of it?" She held the bag up in front of her.

"It keeps bugs out of your kitchen, doesn't it?" He had a vague memory of hearing about it in his biology class or something, but that was it.

"This is food-grade diatomaceous earth, and I want to take it. Any problems with that? A friend of mine takes it and tells me all her joints have stopped aching. I want mine to stop, too."

"Got plans for dancing at the Legion Hall?"

"Don't you put it past me, young man." She gave a sly smile, and Beau barked out a laugh.

"I certainly won't."

"Since Mr. Kinsey died a few years ago I've been known to shake a leg now and then. I just don't want to break a hip while I'm at it, you know?"

"I'll have to check into this a bit further and run it against your medications in our computer program, but at this point I don't see that it will interfere."

"Good—'cause I'm already taking it. At my age, I can't wait around on things."

"Maybe that's why your blood pressure is up, then?" He posed the question.

"Nah. I ran out of my prescription and the pharmacy wouldn't fill it until I came in and you approved it. Sheri's such a stickler for the rules. So approve it. Then I can get on with my life before I have a stroke."

"Mrs. Kinsey, why weren't you this funny when I was in high school?" Beau felt an inappropriate chuckle bubble within him.

"Oh, I was—but back then staff weren't supposed to show they had a sense of humor. Made for some pretty dull classes, I have to say."

"Well, I'm glad you're not holding back now."

He finished the appointment and escorted her and her caregiver out to the front.

"Do you need a follow-up appointment, Mrs. Kinsey?" Aurora asked as they approached the desk, which was amazingly clean for the first time in months. How had she done that so quickly?

"No. She's good," Beau said. "Mrs. Kinsey, I'll call you with the information on any medication interactions."

"Good. If I'm not there leave a message, 'cause I'll probably be out looking for a new dancing dress. There's a sale on this week."

Beau didn't know whether she was serious or not and looked at Aurora, who widened her eyes and shook her head. It was anybody's guess.

"At least she's not driving, right?" Aurora said after the woman and her attendant had left the building.

"No kidding. I don't remember her being so funny when we were in school."

"She wasn't. Seriously."

"But how about this desk? What did you do? Just shove everything into the trash and make it look like you cleaned?"

"No, that's something that *you* would do—not me." She placed her hands on her hips and gave him a serious look.

"Oh, *touché*." But he had to admit she was probably right. He tended to clean with a backhoe.

"I did come up with something I'd like to go over with you."

"Oh, sure—what is it?"

"How about you pull up a chair beside me and we can look at this together? It's for the Brush Valley Day celebration."

"Oh, right." He dragged a chair close to her and settled in to look at the piece of paper in front of them. "Hit me with it. What's your mad plan?"

"My mad plan is to have a booth there all day and reach out to people coming and going. We can offer a blood pressure clinic and be on the lookout for people who are at risk who might need a follow-up. It's also time for flu shots. At the other end of the table we can have that going. Both are ways to get people to stop for a minute and get something for free, which they love, and a quick check that takes less than five minutes. We can have them fill out a form for our information, and we can give *them* some information, too."

With her excitement, her eyes became animated and filled with light, while her hands gestured over the most important points. It was an endearing sight.

"Get something. Give something. Makes sense."

"Exactly. We give them something—the BP check or the shot—and they give us the chance to introduce ourselves to them, tell them about the clinic and make contact with potential new patients."

"Think that will work?"

At this point he had no idea. He didn't like wasting time or resources, but this felt right. Felt good. In this area he had little to no experience, so he was going to have to trust Aurora's instincts.

"Well, sure. Why not? A lot of the people we know are aging. Besides, who wants to go to a town eleven miles away or more through the mountains just to have a flu shot or a checkup when you can get it in your own backyard?" She took a breath, warming to her topic. "Especially in the winter. The roads are treacherous a lot of the time, and people simply won't go when the roads are bad."

"Good point."

He knew his mother hated to drive when the roads were bad, so he had firsthand experience with that. There was no bus or taxi service out here. If you couldn't drive, you were stuck.

"There are all kinds of unhealthy things going

on at the fair, but it brings people in—especially the barbecue chicken at the firemen's booth."

"That's my all-time favorite and it's caused me years of indigestion." Just the memory of it made his mouth water.

"I know—me too. I love the contrast of the firemen using their fire to teach safety to kids and at the same time to cook chicken as their fundraiser."

Beau sat back and thought about her ideas as he looked at the paper and the unreadable notes she'd scribbled all over the notepad.

"I think this is a fabulous idea. Too bad it's too late for us to get into the county fair."

"I can call them and see if there's space— or maybe we could set up shop in the tent with the firemen. They have a spot already, right?"

"They do. Okay. Give them a call and see what you can come up with."

Minute by minute his admiration for her was growing.

"Okay. We've got a lull now for a bit, so I'll do that. What was that you were talking to Mrs. Kinsey about? Something interacting with her medications?"

Those blue eyes of hers looked directly at him and for a second, his heart paused and his mouth went dry. How could an innocent look cause such a reaction in him? Had he been suffering from a lack of female companionship for so long that a look could turn him inside out? He didn't think so and he frowned, turning away from that idea. He was made of sterner stuff than that. He had to resist.

"Oh, yeah. I'll do that now. She was wondering about diatomaceous earth. Ever heard of it?"

A change of topic was a good idea right now. It would keep his mind off what he would do to Aurora if he could.

"No, can't say as I have. What is it?"

"It's an insecticide—"

"*Eww.* And she's taken some?" Horror filled Aurora's eyes.

"No. She wants to take some *food-grade* DE for her aches and pains."

"Wow." She made a face that showed she was interested, but equally puzzled. "Think I'll have to look it up. I have aches and pains too, and as long as I'm not poisoning myself I'd give it a shot."

"Oh, really? My manipulations aren't enough for you?"

Mock horror filled his eyes, and he placed a hand on his heart, as if she'd seriously wounded him there.

"It's not that." A light blush crept from her neck up over her cheeks.

"Then what is it?"

He was teasing her, and thoroughly enjoying the light blush that filled her cheeks. She used to blush a lot in school, and he'd gone out of his way to do or say things that would embarrass her. Now he felt a stirring in his heart that hadn't been there since Julie had died and part of him had died with her.

Maybe that part of him wasn't dead after all... just wounded. Deeply. That was curious and interesting and scary at the same time.

Mrs. Kinsey's words came back to him. It was time. He'd mourned Julie and would never forget her, or how deeply they had loved each other. Was it really time to move on? How was a man to know after a relationship like that? He'd never love that way again. That much he knew. But some part of him was waking up, wanting to connect again.

Aurora had just come back to town. She was here temporarily. He couldn't start depending on her, or start liking having her around so much, or he was going to get his heart broken all over again. He had to think this through with more than one certain body part. Chloe was his number one priority. He couldn't let Aurora into her life and then watch her walk away. *He* could deal with the pain, but he wouldn't put his child through that.

With a frown, he pushed back and stood.

"Never mind. Give the county fair people a call and see if we can get in anywhere."

"Beau? What is it?" She placed a gentle hand on his arm to stop him from walking away. "We were having a good time, then you switched gears and shut down. Did I say something I shouldn't have?"

Those big blue eyes of hers looked up at him like he'd just stabbed her through the heart. He had to remember she had baggage, too. It wasn't just him. Yet that was even more reason not to think of her as anything else except temporary and a friend who was helping him out for a while. So many reasons they shouldn't be together.

"No. Nothing." He looked away and shoved his hands into his pockets. How was he going to explain this to her?

She stood and faced him, her eyes wary but determined. "Now, that's just not true. We both know it. If you're uncomfortable about something it's best to talk about it—not pretend it's not going on or ignore it." She curved one hand behind her ear, the way she did when she was nervous.

"No, you haven't done anything. It's just that—"

The door opened, and they froze.

"Is this the right place?" A middle-aged man

entered and took off his coat. "I can't decide if I'm a dog or a cat today."

At his words the moment between Aurora and Beau was shattered. It was all business again.

"Of course this is the right place." Aurora greeted the man with an overly bright smile. "What can we do for you today?"

Beau waited as she had the man sign in and give her his insurance information. After that Beau led the man back to the patient exam room and focused on the problem in front of him— not on making new ones with Aurora.

Keeping herself busy with filing and organizing took up the majority of Aurora's morning. Although she hadn't quite lied to Beau, she had misrepresented what she'd done in order to clear the desk. She wasn't *that* efficient. What she'd done was put all the piles of paperwork, lab results, faxes and miscellaneous other stuff into two boxes that now sat on the floor at her feet, out of view of the patients. This gave an immediate view of cleanliness and organization—a professional atmosphere a patient would feel comfortable in.

After that she'd cleaned the surface of the desk, so she had a clutter-free, dust-free surface to work on. Clutter, she understood. Dirt, she had a personal problem with.

Now that everything was clean she began to go through the papers, sorting them into piles: letters that needed to have copies mailed to patients, information that might need a phone call for follow-up, before being scanned into the electronic medical records. All things that made a good first impression on new patients.

After an hour of sitting in the chair, the pain began in her hips and she stood. With her hands on her hips she arched her back, looking at the ceiling. This was a stretch she'd learned in physical therapy.

"Looks like you'll be good as new if you keep up the exercises—and no more lifting things you shouldn't," Beau said to his patient as they came through the clinic door.

"I know. I'm finally going to have to admit I'm not as young as I used to be."

The patient walked out with Beau.

"That's true. But here's your chance to delegate authority, Vern. You're the *owner* of the company. You don't have to tote every beam or bag of cement yourself. Get some of those young guys to do the heavy lifting."

"Good point, Beau."

Vern walked a little straighter as he left the office, and saluted Aurora on the way out.

"Are most of your patients here for adjustments?" she asked as she worked on another stretch.

"Maybe about fifty percent. There's a chiropractor in Indiana, but he's usually swamped, so I get his leftovers." A shrug lifted his shoulders. "Works for me for now."

"Wow. Maybe that's something you should put on your advertising, too. After studying your appointment calendar, it looks like you can usually get people in the same day. That would be a major selling point for people who need an adjustment quickly. Like Vern, there. He just walked in and you were able to see him. Maybe we could set aside one or two appointments every day for emergency adjustments."

"That's a great idea. Are you *sure* you aren't a marketer disguised as a nurse?"

"Oh, no." She laughed, and stretched her back to one side then the other. "I guess I could be called an opportunist. When there's an opportunity that presents itself, I jump on it."

"Very observant."

He stepped closer to her and her senses went on high alert. After their last conversation had fizzled, she wasn't sure what to expect as he neared.

"*I'm* being very observant right now," he said.

"What are you seeing?"

She was seeing him very close, and observing that the hairs on her arms were going up, alerted like she was in a dangerous situation. Only this situation was dangerous to her senses.

"I'm seeing that you need a break. Your back is bothering you, isn't it?"

"Yes…but it's okay."

"No, it's not. You had your hands on your hips in a classic sore back posture. Take a break. That paperwork isn't going anywhere."

"There are lab reports that need to be looked at." Proving her worth to him was extremely important to her. "I don't want you to replace me already because I'm slacking on the job."

"That's just not possible. I'll look at them." Beau glanced down at Daisy, who cast her eyes in adoration up to him. "Maybe you can take Daisy out back for a walk along the edge of the pasture. She hasn't been out since we got here."

"Oh, good plan."

She looked down at the dog on its bed and her heart cramped a little. Beau had had his perfect world and then it had been shattered.

"Do dogs grieve, I wonder?"

"What?"

"Oh, God. I said that out loud, didn't I?" How humiliating.

"Yes, you did. What made you think about that right now?"

A puzzled expression covered his face. Then

it was closed, and she hoped she hadn't offended him.

"I was just thinking of you and how your world was broken up when your wife died and I wondered if Daisy misses her, too."

The ache in her chest was twofold. One for him and one for his daughter, who had never known her mother at all. Tragedy was everywhere, and never closer to home than at this moment.

"Well. Yes." He cleared his throat and looked away, obviously uncomfortable with the topic. "I think dogs *do* grieve. Daisy wouldn't eat for a week, and she slept on Julie's side of the bed until she realized Julie wasn't coming home again." He sighed. "After that, she slept on the floor beside me. Hasn't gotten back up onto the bed since."

"Beau..."

She held her arms out to him as tears filled her eyes. It was still painful—that was obvious—and she hadn't meant to bring up anything to open the wound for him. But sometimes that was what friends did, they helped each other to heal. They dug at the hard stuff until it was all out in the light.

"I'm so sorry."

Beau wrapped his arms around her and they held on to each other for a few minutes. No words were spoken. None were needed in order for them to communicate. She felt the trembling in his body and it was echoed in her own. The pain he was in was *real*.

Daisy nudged at their legs with her nose and pushed with her head until Aurora pulled back with a watery laugh. "I see. You need to go out, don't you, girl?"

"Thanks. I needed a hug and didn't even know it."

"We all do, Beau. It's up to our friends to point it out now and then."

She stepped back before that haunted look in his eyes overwhelmed her and she took a step past her boundaries that she'd regret. They were friends, and if she gave in to the impulse to be more, their friendship, and their work relationship would be changed forever. She didn't want that. She didn't need it right now. She needed him as a friend, and she needed this job more than anything. That was all it had to be for her, or she wouldn't be able to carry on working here.

She snapped her fingers at Daisy. "Let's go, girl. I think we both need a walk."

But before she could open the door Beau caught her by the arm, pulled her back toward him.

"Wait. Just a second."

* * *

"What?"

The second her blue eyes met his, Beau felt something cramp in his chest. The pace of his heart was usually strong and even, but now he felt like a kid with a crush. He didn't know what it was, but he knew he couldn't let her walk out the door without saying something to her.

It was just a walk. Just taking the dog out. Only a few minutes away from him. But something pulled at him. A connection. That was what he needed—a connection. Heat burned in his chest in a way that he hadn't felt for a long time, and he wasn't comfortable with it now, but he was powerless to resist it.

"Um…" What was wrong with him?

"Beau? Are you okay?"

Concern filled her eyes as she looked at him. Though she still held her body stiffly. It was probably because she'd become used to holding herself that way. She leaned toward him and her eyes showed her interest.

What would happen if she reached out to him the way he wanted to reach out to her?

CHAPTER SEVEN

"I'M OKAY. I just…just wanted to tell you how much I appreciate you being here with me, helping me. Us." He glanced down at Daisy. "Helping us get our lives back together."

Why was it so hard to admit that? That he needed help. That he needed *her*.

That made her smile, and his heart fell into place. Despite all of his precautions, his vow to be self-protective, that smile of hers was sending him over the edge.

"It's okay, Beau. You're helping me, too."

"A mutually beneficial arrangement, then—right?"

The smile she flashed at him created a thrumming in his chest where the heat had just been.

"Right. Guess we'd better go before she gets impatient." She opened it and the dog dashed through it. "We'll be right back. You're on phone duty!"

A short while later the two of them returned.

Daisy dashed through the door and leaped up into his arms like she'd done when she was a puppy. Now, with seventy pounds of grown dog flying through the air, he wasn't ready for it. At the last second he made a grab for her, and they both landed on the floor amidst kisses and licks and happy dog slobber all over his face.

He laughed. He tried to capture her collar and drag her off him, but the dog wasn't going to be deterred. She stood on his chest and then lay down on him, so happy to see him, although she'd been gone only a few minutes.

Another laugh erupted from his gut, and then another. Before he knew it tears of laughter and joy that he hadn't shed for a long time fell from his eyes and down his cheeks. He pulled Daisy against him and caught his breath. She whined once, then settled against him on the floor.

Aurora's hand touched his shoulder, and her touch, her energy, her compassion all reached out to him. He took her hand in his. Lying on the floor with Daisy and Aurora, he didn't feel silly, but for some reason he just felt loved.

"Are you okay?"

The tone of her voice was different. Quietly questioning. She wanted to engage him, he knew, but didn't want to pry into his emotions. She was such a compassionate woman, and totally perfect as his office nurse. Somehow, lying there on the floor, being suffocated by his dog, Aurora's beautiful caramel blonde hair all tousled, he decided he needed to figure out a way to keep Aurora with him.

Permanently.

"I'm good. I haven't felt this good in a long time."

His breath wheezed in and out of his throat. Daisy seemed to have pushed out all the heavy stuff that he'd kept locked inside and each new breath he took pushed out stagnant air and brought more life into him.

"We used to do this when she was a puppy. She must have had a memory strike her, or something, 'cause she hasn't done that in ages." He cupped Aurora's hand in one of his and massaged Daisy's ear with the other. "This is the kind of greeting everyone should have. From someone who loves them unconditionally— don't you think?"

"Absolutely." She sniffed. "There hasn't been much of that in my life, Beau. Seems like the people who loved me only loved me for the things I did for them, not because I was a cool person or anything." She rubbed Daisy's back. "Maybe I need a dog, too."

"That's so wrong." He turned his head to look at her, though she was upside down. "You *are* a cool person, and you deserve so much more than that."

Hesitating for just a second, he brought her hand to his lips and kissed it. That was as far as he could go right now. Though he wanted to reach out to her, there were so many reasons he shouldn't. So much was at stake for both of them.

"Now you're really going to make me cry." She wiped her face with the back of her hand just as the bell over the front door rang, admitting another patient.

Abandoning her human pillow, Daisy trotted over to the door to see what was going on. Fearful that she might jump up and injure a patient, Beau opened his mouth to call her. Before he could do that Aurora snapped her fingers once and ordered the dog to sit—which Daisy quickly did, then offered a paw.

A squeal of delight shattered the peaceful air as Beau picked himself up off the floor. He held a hand out to Aurora and assisted her to a standing position.

"Down. *Down!*"

An impatient little girl of about four years old, with wild blonde curls, struggled from the grip of her father.

He looked at Beau and Aurora while holding on to the struggling child. "Is it okay?"

"Oh, yes. Daisy's good with children."

"Good, 'cause this kid loves dogs." The dad grinned and shook his head. "Every single stuffed animal she has is a dog."

The father set her down and the girl immediately fell to the floor in front of Daisy, as if worshiping her, then hugged the dog's sturdy neck. Daisy just sat, as if she knew what to do, as if she knew this was her purpose in life—to be hugged by kids and to love them.

Beau offered the sign-in sheet to the man. "You new around here? You don't look familiar."

"I am—but she's not. My wife, Dana, usually brings her in, but today it's my job." He ruffled his daughter's hair with affection. "Needs a booster shot of some sort. Dana said you'd have it in the records in case I forgot—which I did."

"No problem." Beau took a quick look at the sheet for the name and handed the clipboard back to Aurora. "I'll grab her chart."

After the shot was administered, and the requisite ear-piercing scream had lifted the hair on his arms, Beau led them back to the front desk.

"Daisy gives good hugs if you need another one." He crouched down to talk to the little girl with big, tearful eyes. "Nurse Aurora might have a lollipop for you, too."

After a few seconds of consideration, apparently deciding between crying or hugging the dog, she nodded and hurried over to Daisy for another hug.

Aurora gave the treat to her dad. "You might want to keep it, or it's going to have dog hair on it."

"I'll do that." He tucked the lollipop in his shirt pocket. "Come on, Misty. Say goodbye to Daisy."

"Aw…" she said and shook her head, setting her curls to bouncing. "But I *like* Daisy." Casting a pair of soulful blue eyes on her father, Misty tried her best to linger a while with the dog.

"I know. But Daisy will be here next time you visit." He looked at Beau. "Right, Doc?"

"For sure." He turned to Aurora. "Decision made. Daisy is the official mascot for the clinic."

"Good decision," she said, and then her gaze skittered away from him.

He'd noticed she hadn't sat down since coming back into the clinic.

"I'm thinking I need to go upstairs and lie down for a while…if you can handle the clinic for an hour or two?"

"Your back? Or something else?"

Though he'd just kissed her hand, he really wanted to kiss her lips, and she probably knew it. He hoped she wasn't uncomfortable with him now. That was something he didn't need, hadn't intended, and certainly didn't want. But he still wanted to do it.

"Yes. It's the chair, I think. Sitting for so long puts too much pressure on my back in the wrong places."

"Got it. Maybe we can put some sort of support into it for you."

"That would be nice—but don't go to any fuss, Beau. This is a pain I'm going to have to learn to live with, I think."

The change in her face was obvious. The bright, sunny features that had been there moments ago now held disappointment.

"Go. We'll be fine."

Daisy followed her to the doorway, then looked back at him, as if trying to tell him he needed to do something, but he let her go. She needed the peace right now and, frankly, so did he.

He snapped his fingers the way Aurora had, and Daisy returned to sit at his feet. He dropped into the desk chair and quickly scanned the schedule. There was an empty hour, with no one coming in. If no one dropped by he could get the task he had in mind done in no time.

He opened an internet browser and clicked on the local office supply warehouse to see what they had in stock.

He had a sudden need to upgrade his office chairs.

* * *

Aurora could delay only so long before she had to go back down to the clinic. After having lunch and lying down for a bit she felt the spasm in her back ease, as if someone had pulled on the end of a bow to unravel it. Now she felt great, and had no excuse not to see Beau.

If she were being honest with herself she had to admit that there had been a moment between them—a special moment—when Beau had looked at her in a way he'd never done before, and she'd responded in a way she'd never done before, either. But there were so many reasons not to give in to her desires, not to let herself feel things for Beau. This new situation, this new phase of her life, could all go down the drain in a heartbeat if things didn't work out between them.

Could she risk their friendship, risk her new job and stability, for something that wasn't a sure thing? Right now, she couldn't. There was *never* a sure thing when it came to relationships.

Plastering a smile on her face, she opened the back door to the clinic and found Beau on the floor, his legs splayed out at awkward angles. Alarm cut right through her, and her heart raced erratically. But Daisy lay quietly beside him, not bothered, so Aurora paused a second.

Beside Beau was a box. A very large box with a picture of a chair on the side.

"What…?" She took a few steps forward. "Beau? What are you doing?"

"Can you hand me that screwdriver? It said flathead, but it's a Phillips. I don't know who writes the instructions for this stuff, but they need a new job."

He pointed to the twelve-inch tool with its hefty black and yellow handle. Stooping down, she handed it to him.

"As you can see, I'm putting together a chair."

"But why?"

He looked at her and blinked, as if she'd said something crazy. "Because you need one."

"Oh, Beau. You didn't have to do that."

No one had ever done anything like that for her, and a little flutter of warmth shot through her heart, tearing down those flimsy little barriers she'd just put up.

"Sure I did. The other one was giving your back trouble, so this is an easy fix. Your back's happy, you're happy. You're happy, I'm happy."

"Simple as that?"

"Simple as that."

Beau turned the screw a few more times. "Done." He rolled over and jumped to his feet. "Here. Take it for a spin."

A ridiculous bubble of pleasure pulsed inside her chest. "Well, okay. If you insist."

"I insist."

He put one hand on the chair to steady it, and with a sweeping gesture of his other hand offered it to her. With a giggle she sat, and Beau pushed her over to the desk.

"How's it feel?"

Aurora wiggled her hips, trying to decide how the chair fit her.

With excitement in her eyes, she looked up at him. "It's great."

"Awesome."

He spun her around in a circle and then put his hands on the arms of the chair to stop it. Her face was only inches from his, and the second he looked down at her mouth that familiar zing shot through her system.

God, she wanted his hands on her, his mouth on hers, his skin against hers. His head slowly lowered, his lips aiming to claim hers. Could she kiss him? Should she kiss him? She wanted to. But what about their friendship, his daughter, her temporary life here...?

Aurora shook her head, the heady fog clearing somewhat. There was too much at stake. She took a deep breath. "I know we're not teenagers, Beau. But this thing that's happening between us is so new—"

He stooped, so she didn't have to look up at him and crane her neck. "I know. For me, too. We've never looked at each other this way before. It's crazy. It's exciting. It's scary."

He blew out a sigh and placed one hand over hers, but didn't back away from this conversation that was difficult for both of them.

"But if we don't reach out, take a step that's scary, we'll never know, will we?"

Unable to stop herself, she placed her right hand on his cheek and looked into his eyes. "You've been through some tough times...you have a child and a business now. Your life's complicated." She looked down, uncertain how to say what she wanted to say to him. "I'm so ruined, I don't know if I can find my way back. You shouldn't—"

"Don't tell me what I should and shouldn't feel." After placing his hand beneath her chin, he raised her face to his and waited until she looked at him. "You're not ruined, Aurora. You've hit a pothole in the road. That's all. And I'm... I don't know what I am...but right now I really want to kiss you."

He leaned in, and this time she met him halfway.

She paused for a second, savoring the feelings swirling inside, trying to decide whether this was a good idea or not, but curiosity and need won over any caution whispering in her ears.

When his lips touched hers she opened up to him and met his tongue with her own. The soft, silky glide stirred feelings in the pit of her stomach, in her feminine flesh, that hadn't stirred in entirely too long. He held her face as if she were precious, and fragile, and important, and beautiful.

Tears sprang to her eyes. She pulled back, her breathing coming fast, her heart thrumming in her chest.

"I didn't mean to make you cry. Was it that bad?" A sideways smile lifted Beau's mouth.

"No, you goof. In fact it was quite the opposite. You made me feel things I haven't in a long time."

"That's good, then—right?" He eased back down to kneel in front of her.

"I don't know, Beau. This is so strange and wonderful all at once, and I've no experience with it."

None at all. There were so many reasons not to go down this road with Beau. Had they already gone too far?

"Me, either. We're both on new and unfamiliar ground. All we can do is see if we're a good match, other than as friends, and go from there."

"There's so much about me you don't know."

That worried her. She'd changed so much from the old days. So had he.

With a gentle hand he pushed her hair back from her face. "There's a lot of me that you don't know either, and I'd like you to." He closed his eyes and cleared his throat. "I'd like to tell you about my wife sometime, too."

"I'd like that." With hands that trembled a bit she cupped his face, brought him closer for a light, tender kiss. He didn't try to take it any further than that. "But for now we have a business to run, and you've got a baby to go get in a few minutes."

"You're right." He stepped back, still watching her, considering. "We'll need to revisit this conversation another time, but tomorrow how about you tell me some more of your ideas for Brush Valley Day? I think you're really onto something there."

"I will. I have a notebook full of stuff."

He kept backing toward the door, watching her until he'd backed into the wall and stumbled before gaining his feet.

Without taking his gaze from her, he reached behind him for the door. "I'll see you tomorrow."

"Tomorrow, then."

She sighed, her heart pulsing with a new warmth as he left.

"Wow. Just *wow*."

Grabbing her keys and her purse, she turned off the lights in the main room just as the door opened.

"I'm sorry, but we're— Beau! What are you doing? Did you forget something?"

"Uh, yeah." He emitted a sharp whistle. "Kinda forgot my dog."

Daisy trotted out from beneath the desk and went to Beau.

"Oh, dear. Glad you remembered her."

"Yes. I was a little distracted there for a few minutes."

"Glad you're better now."

That little hum in her chest hummed a little faster, a little warmer and a little louder, and the warning bells faded away into the distance.

This was a new and very interesting development in their relationship.

The tremor in her hands still hadn't receded when she reached for the phone after Beau left. The time had come for her to call in reinforcements.

Tammie had been her friend forever. They'd been pals since first grade. No matter when she called Tammie, they could have a conversation like they'd seen each other yesterday. That was a sign of true friendship.

"Hey, girlfriend!"

Tammie answered the phone with her usual exuberance. The blue-eyed redhead always had a big smile and a quick joke whenever Aurora needed it.

"Hey."

After chatting for a minute, Aurora finally admitted her reason for calling.

"I have a problem, and I need to talk. Do you have time to listen and offer some advice?"

"Oh, absolutely. Is this an I-need-popcorn kind of chat, or an I-need-booze-and-ice cream talk?"

"I'm thinking it's somewhere in the middle." It wasn't that bad, but it wasn't that good either. "Can you meet me at the coffee shop?"

"Sure. Be there in twenty minutes…"

After settling in at the coffee shop with their choice of beverages, Tammie got the conversation rolling.

"Okay, shoot. What's going on? You sounded stressed out on the phone."

Aurora blew out a breath, took another one, and then filled her friend in on the dilemma of Beau and their mutual attraction.

"I don't want to start something if I'm only going to leave here and go back to Virginia, but I don't want to go back to Virginia if I've started something here!"

How convoluted was *that*? Of course hearing the words out loud made things sound way worse than in her head.

"You sound very confused about it."

Tammie always got to the heart of a situation quickly. That was what made her a great friend and an awesome therapist.

"I am. I can't believe it. I'm usually the level-headed one and you're the wild child."

"Oh, really?" Tammie's delicate brows rose at that statement.

"Yes, really. Like you don't remember."

Aurora relaxed as she reminded her friend of how many times she'd come home intoxicated or taken a horseback ride through town at midnight. Naked.

"I guess you're right. But in all of my adventures what I gained was perspective."

"It's that perspective I need now."

Seriously. There was no one else she could go to.

"Go for it."

Tammie gave the simple advice and sipped her green tea.

"What do you mean?" Had she heard correctly? "Go for it? With Beau?"

"I mean *go for it*. Everything. There's no sense in going back to Virginia when you'll be wondering if you gave up the chance of a lifetime here. You'll regret it if you don't at least try, right?" Tammie adjusted her position. "For me, I don't want to be on my deathbed and say, *'I wish I had...'* How about you?"

"No. No, I don't." Aurora paused and thought a minute. "That's one way to look at it. But is it too late already? I mean, will Julie be a ghost between us forever? Will he think about her every time he looks at Chloe?" Hesitation swirled in her abdomen. "Another way to look at the situation is, what if we go for it, it goes badly, and we lose our friendship? That would make me so sad."

Tammie placed her warm hand over Aurora's. "You could both win, too. If you stay without at least giving it a shot you'll both be frustrated, which can ruin a relationship in a whole other way."

"That's yet another way to look at it." She slapped her hands on the sides of her head and closed her eyes. "God! This is so hard. What do I *do*?"

"Take a breath. Relax and let it go. It's only hard if you try to control it. If you let things unfold naturally it's much better. If you think about things too much—and you *do*—you'll end up with a big, fat headache."

"Yeah. My special brand of self-torture."

She leaned back in the chair and stared at her

friend as if the answers would come flooding out her mouth.

"You really need to relax. Why don't you take one of my yoga classes? It helps a lot."

"Beau mentioned yoga for my back, but it might help me with everything else, too."

"It's mind-body-spirit therapy. Can't get any more comprehensive than that." Tammie gave a sharp nod. "Might help you get off the pain medications, too."

Decision made.

"I can use all of that. Still at the community center, right?"

The place had been built after Aurora had left for Virginia. In the center of the little town, it was a gathering place for many people and many reasons.

"Right. Check the website for class times. I can't keep track of all the days and times in my head." She waved a hand, dismissing the idea.

"Thanks, Tam. I appreciate you listening."

Over the years she'd had other girlfriends, but none like her old friend from home. The thought occurred to her that if she remained in Brush Valley she could see Tammie more often, too. That would be a wonderful thing.

"So, what are you going to do?" Tammie watched Aurora with interest. "I can keep a secret."

"I don't know, but I'm not going to give up…
on any of it…just because it's difficult."

"There you go. You came up with your own
answer. When you let go of security, of things
that are familiar, that's where growth occurs.
Sometimes answers."

"So, you're an old sage now?"

Those wise words coming from Tammie, who
seemed not to have a care in the world, had surprised Aurora.

"No. My yoga teacher is. I learned that from
her." Tammie sighed. "I hated that advice when
I first heard it, but now I know it's the truth. You
just have to find a way to let go of the old and
embrace the new. Drop what no longer serves
you."

"Great. Right now I don't know what's old
and what's new, and if I let go of anything I'm
just hoping there's a net when I fall."

Tammie leaned forward, her eyes intense and
looking wise beyond her years. "You have to
trust that you don't *need* a net. That's the key."

"How do I *know* that?" Panic flashed through
her at the thought of not having a new stronghold before leaving the old one.

"There's only one way to find out, right?"

"By letting go? *Completely?* But it's so scary.
I hate being scared."

Right now her heart was going on a marathon race in her chest.

"Life *is* scary, my friend."

"I thought you were supposed to be giving me support and telling me lies, saying that everything is going to be okay."

"Everything *is* going to be okay. It just may not be in the way you imagine it right now. That's no lie."

"I still have a life to get back to in Virginia."

Didn't she? Wasn't that where she belonged?

"Isn't that what I worked so hard to find? If I stay here, doesn't that mean I've given up on my dreams?"

"Says who?" Tammie leaned back in her chair, cradling her cup of green tea. "What makes you think your life is in Virginia any longer?"

"Are you *serious*?" Aurora's eyes popped wide. "I had a job in Virginia, I had a life there until a car crash took it all away from me. I want that life back." A cramp tugged at her heart. "Don't I...?"

"Listen to yourself. You *had* those things. *Had.* Perhaps the universe is telling you that you need a different life now, and it took the crash to kick you out of what you *thought* you needed." Tammie nodded. "You learned what you needed to learn there, and now it's time to move on."

"That crash almost killed me." The words were a whisper coming from her soul and tears clouded her vision. "I can't give up, Tammie. I *can't*."

"It's not giving up. It's redefining what you want out of life. There's no shame in that. Some lessons are harder than others. Sometimes we don't listen to the signs until something this traumatic happens. This was a wake-up call and you need to listen."

"How do I know I'm not making a royal mistake by not returning to my old life?"

"You *can't* return to your old life."

"What?" Startled, Aurora widened her eyes.

"It's gone—and I'm wondering if that old Aurora, so determined to not need anyone, is gone too."

Before Aurora could protest, Tammie held up a hand.

"Think about it. Think about what you really want in life. Do you want marriage, a family, friends and a community, or do you want independence, to have work be your life?"

"Can't be both, can it?" Aurora's shoulders dropped. Those were straight, honest words and it was a concept she hadn't considered before.

"Not usually. We can't have it all. We have to

pick the things that work the best and leave the rest behind." She shrugged and her silk shawl slid from her shoulder. "Besides, do you *really* want it all? Having it all comes with a lot of responsibilities."

"I suppose so."

Her friends in Virginia had come from a variety of places, but the one thing they'd all had in common was that they were driven. Was that *her* anymore? Did she want a simpler life now?

An image of Chloe popped into her mind. She was such a beautiful baby, with her green eyes and blonde hair so like her father's, and Aurora already wanted to be around her more. Maybe one day have a child of her own.

"Just think about it—see how things go. Maybe write down the pros and cons of each. Seeing it on paper might help."

"I'll try it."

Tammie half closed her eyelids and appeared to be listening to something other than Aurora's voice. Maybe she was listening to the universe.

"Tammie?"

"Yes, sorry." She leaned forward across the table and took both of Aurora's hands in hers. "You go get 'em. Listen to your instincts and your heart. They can't both be wrong at the same time, right? Call if you need me."

"Are you going to be around this weekend?"

Without answering right away, Tammie tilted her head to the side and gave an enigmatic smile. She could be a redheaded Mona Lisa.

"Uncertain. I have a date with an artist in Pittsburgh on Friday. The weekend could go anywhere after that."

"You go, girl!"

Aurora laughed and some of the tension lifted. They chatted for a while longer over another cup, parting ways with a hug and an agreement to meet the next week.

After talking to Tammie she felt better. Sharing her burden, her fears and anxieties had helped. Reconnecting with an old friend had helped, too. Not trying to keep everything tied up inside made her feel lighter in the chest.

The drive back to her little apartment took her past the road leading to her mother's house, but she kept going. Right now there wasn't enough time to have a visit. Maybe tomorrow she would stop. With her mother, there was never a short phone call or a short visit.

CHAPTER EIGHT

SEVERAL BUSY WEEKS passed at the clinic, with a flurry of people coming in for school check-ups, and sports physicals, and a variety of the ailments that were the lifeblood of Beau's office. The appointments calendar was getting fuller every day, making Beau very happy. And working with Aurora was the icing on the cake.

"Seems like word is getting out about the clinic. It must be the perfect location. People drive by and realize it's here."

That was proof, as far as he was concerned, of the good choice he'd made in location.

Aurora chewed her lip and a worried look came into her eyes. "I may have dropped some informational fliers at the community center."

"*May* have? You don't know?"

Hmm...

"Well, yes... I do know." She cringed.

"So, did you or didn't you?"

"I did. I'm sorry. I signed up for Tammie's yoga class and thought while I was there I'd see if they had room to promote local businesses, and they did."

"That's great." He definitely approved of the way her mind worked.

"And the library and the post office, too."

"Seriously?" Dumbfounded, he stared at her.

"That's where people around here can be found. And in the fire hall, too. *Ooh!* I hadn't thought of that one. Let me put it on my list."

She opened a drawer of the desk and pulled out a large yellow notepad, flipped through several pages of notes and scribbled another one at the end.

"That's your list of ideas?"

Beau was impressed. He thought she'd have a few notes jotted down on a sticky pad—not an entire notebook filled with ideas.

"It's a manifesto."

"Yes. I'm sorry." She clutched it to her chest, eyes filled with worry. "Is it too much? Have I overstepped?"

"I don't know yet." He held out his hand. "Let's have a look at it."

Hesitating for a second, Aurora placed it in his hands. "Why don't you sit down and I can explain it to you? You might not understand my scribbling."

"Okay." He grabbed the old desk chair and scooted it close to her. "Tell me about your ideas."

Aurora leaned closer to him and her fragrance washed over him. It was a subtle mix of spice, maybe sandalwood, that stirred his senses, and the words on the pages blurred. He stopped trying to focus on the pad and just listened to the excitement in her voice, let her fragrance wash through his mind.

Her ideas rolled in his brain, and he was intrigued by the way her mind worked, how she had come up with a marketing plan for opportunities he'd never even thought of.

"So that's it." She closed the pad and her eagerness showed in her eyes.

"That's it? That's *all* you've got?"

He was teasing her, and enjoyed the flustered look on her face.

"Well, I haven't had much time to focus on it lately, but—"

"Relax, Aurora. I'm just giving you a hard time. You've done more in a few weeks than I could have done in months." A bubble of pleasure churned inside him. "I *knew* working with you was going to be awesome."

Every day there was something new, something interesting. Some new burst of life that made him want to enjoy, to live fully again. Yet guilt surfaced right after, to dull the edges and pull him backward.

The bubble he'd been living in burst.

"What's wrong? I can see it on your face." She took a big breath. "Are you having second thoughts? About a lot of things?"

Without answering, he stood and walked a few steps away. Her nearness, her fragrance, the easy way they worked together shook him to a depth he didn't think he was ready for.

"No. It's nothing."

"Stop it." She stood and faced him, anger snapping in her eyes, in the posture she took as she faced him. "Right now."

"Aurora, I don't think this is the time—"

"Yes, it is. Right here. Right now. If you can't face moving on, that's fine. If you're having feelings for me that you're having difficulty with, that's fine too. But don't shut me out— because it's not my fault, and yet you're punishing me. You have been for weeks. Ever since…"

Their kiss.

For a few seconds he stared at her. There was truth in her face, in her eyes, and he knew it. There were questions. There would always be questions. But if he didn't at least try to take a step forward, he'd never get anywhere.

"You're right." He blew out a breath. "Admitting that is hard for me, Aurora. Very hard. But you're exactly right. You don't deserve to take the brunt of my pain."

"We all have pain, Beau. But if you share it, even a little bit, it doesn't hurt as much, you know."

An encouraging smile lifted her lips, but a bruised uncertainty still filled her eyes and that he couldn't take. *He* was responsible for putting it there.

"I'm sorry." He pulled her against him. "I know I'm all over the place with this, but I'm coming to depend on you so much, so quickly, it's frightening."

"I'm with you—but we have to be able to communicate about things, whatever comes up. I don't want to wonder what you're thinking or what I've done wrong."

"I understand what you're saying. But sometimes the best thing seems to be to keep quiet, when that's really not the best thing at all."

"So from here on out let's really try—"

At that moment the shrieking sound of car tires skidding on pavement tore their attention away. They clung to each other for a few seconds, both cringing, waiting to see if there would be a crash.

There was.

The impact of the crash shook the building

like an earthquake. They all jumped, including Daisy, who cowered beneath the desk.

"Oh, boy. That didn't sound good." Beau grabbed her hand. "Come on."

Together they dashed out the door.

Beau wasn't a trauma doctor, but he and Aurora were the best bet as first responders. A small car had missed the sharp turn in front of the clinic and crashed head-on into a utility pole right beside the building. No wonder the impact had shaken the whole place.

"Oh, my God. Beau!"

Aurora squeezed his hand, then raced around the other side of the car, looking in through the broken window.

"Three people."

"I'll try to get the driver's door open. Can you turn off the ignition? I can't reach it from here."

"Yes."

Since the passenger window was broken, she was able to turn off the ignition, hopefully preventing any sort of electrical fire in the engine.

"I'll call 911 now."

She pulled her phone out and made the call for emergency assistance. Out in this area of the county most rescue services were volunteers, so help wasn't mere minutes away as in larger cities. Out here people depended on their neighbors, friends and Good Samaritans to help out in emergencies.

Beau focused on the handle of the driver's door. It was an old car, and he pushed the handle down and tugged. The metal was twisted and crunched. There was no way he was getting anyone out through this door without heavy machinery.

The driver moaned and raised a hand to his head. A teenager, with two friends in the car, he'd probably been talking, and distracted, and hadn't realized the curve was so sharp.

"Aurora? Go grab a few blankets or sheets. I want to cover the driver so I can push the glass out."

"Got it. This one's still out, has a bump on the head, but that's all I can see right now. The girl in the back is unconscious, too."

She gave him her quick assessment, then ran back into the clinic.

Tugging on the door again brought no better results than his previous attempt, but he couldn't just stand there and do nothing. He'd had to stand by and watch his wife die while he did nothing. That was *not* going to happen here. Here he could help, he could rescue, and he could save lives.

A car horn beeped and a large pickup truck

made a quick turn into the parking lot and stopped beside them.

"Hey, looks like you need some help." One of his old classmates, Robby Black, hurried over. "Did it just happen?"

"Yes. I can't get the door open." In an example of frustration, he yanked on the door again, but it still didn't move.

"I got a crowbar in the truck…" Robby made the offer as he stared at the mangled car.

"Get it."

There was no time to waste.

Aurora rushed from the building, her arms full of linens and an emergency kit, just as Robby arrived with the pry bar.

"Aurora, cover them the best you can with the sheets. If the glass goes flying it will protect them."

"Got it."

While Aurora set about her task, Beau and Robby set the end of the steel rod in the buckled edge of the driver's door.

"On three."

Together they used their combined strength to try and pry the door open, but it wasn't budging.

"Again."

They tried again, but their effort was still futile. The door was not going to move.

"Why don't you try the back door? Maybe it's not as bad."

Aurora made the suggestion and the men moved the tool to the back door—and popped it open on the first try.

"Awesome…"

The young female was rousing from her slumped position.

"At least she's buckled in."

Together Beau and Robby extricated the girl and placed her on a blanket on the ground, away from the vehicle.

"Aurora, stay with her and keep her head in alignment while we try to get the front passenger door open."

More people had stopped their cars, seeing the increased activity.

Two people Beau knew from the pharmacy hurried over. "Can we help out?"

"Yes. Relieve Aurora so she can come over here with us."

"Got it."

In a few minutes Aurora returned to his side. "What do you need me to do?"

As the physician, he was in charge of the scene until rescue services arrived and everyone looked to him for direction—even Aurora.

"We're going to try to get this door open and take them out this way. Can you get into the backseat and hold onto his head, keep him still while we work on the door?"

"Yes."

Aurora climbed into the backseat on the passenger side and placed her hands on the sides of the passenger's head, holding it steady.

"Ready here."

"One, two, three—go."

The door popped open with just two forceful applications of the crowbar.

"We need to get him out, but I want to immobilize his neck."

"Do you have any collars in the clinic?" Aurora asked.

"No. None." He'd never thought he'd need those kinds of supplies.

"How about some towels and tape? We can use them to make a soft collar."

"Brilliant. You stay here and I'll go get them."

"I can go."

"You're already in position."

"Beau, it's my back…"

A twinge of pain crossed her face. Though she'd tried to hide it, he was glad she'd spoken up before letting it get too far.

"I'll relieve you."

He placed his hands on the young man's head, over top of Aurora's, and she slid her hands out from under his. Looking over the seat at her, he saw her meet his gaze with determination shining. She was so good at this. So good. The woman could do anything.

"I've got him now. Go."

With the help of the little band of people who had stopped by they were able to safely extricate all three youths from the car, and then the ambulance crew and paramedics arrived, just behind the fire truck.

"What do we have going on here?" Randy Overdorff, the chief of the fire group, bailed off the truck even before it had come to a halt.

"Looks like they took the turn too fast. Three in the car, all with injuries, all three with loss of consciousness. Two have awakened."

Beau gave the assessment as he watched Aurora placing an IV in the third victim.

"Got it," Randy said, then gave a slow whistle as his brows shot up. "How did you get them out of that mess without hydraulics?"

"Crowbar," Beau said.

"And muscle," Robby added, and flexed both of his arms like a champion wrestler.

"Good going. We'll call for another ambulance from Armagh and they can take one in. We'll get the first two."

Randy spoke into a handheld radio, calling for backup from the small town of Armagh, just four miles away. Armagh was like Brush Valley. A wide spot in the road where people had settled, opened a few businesses and called it home.

The next two hours passed in a flurry of activity as the three teenagers were taken to hospital, the scene investigation was completed, and a tow truck hauled the car away. Beau took a few seconds to text Ginny that he'd be late picking up Chloe.

"Someone's going to have to call the utility company about the pole."

Looking exhausted, Aurora sat on a landscaping rock beside the door of the clinic. Until now, he hadn't noticed how pale and drawn she was. This event had taken its toll on her and he hadn't noticed.

"Already on it," Randy said. "They'll be out in the morning to work on repairs. Meantime, looks like you're closed until that can be done."

The fire chief stood beside Beau with a clipboard full of notes.

"Oh, boy. Does that include the apartment?" Aurora asked.

"Afraid so." Beau looked up at the apartment window. "Hadn't thought of that."

"I guess I could go stay with my mother— or light a few candles." She took a deep breath in, resolving herself to the issue. "I'll be fine."

"I'll leave you to it, then." Randy saluted.

"Thanks, Chief."

Though he spoke to the man climbing onto the fire truck, Beau kept his gaze on Aurora. The longer he watched her, the angrier he got. He'd been so focused he'd completely forgotten about her medical condition, and she'd said nothing. *Nothing.* Not until she was in great pain.

"Aurora?" He approached her, his steps stiff and rigid. He couldn't seem to make himself relax.

"Hi, there." She looked up at him from her position on the rock, and couldn't hide the wince the movement caused. "What a day. Sure ended with a bang, didn't it?"

"We need to talk. Let's go inside."

"What? What's wrong? What did I do?"

Dammit. His temper was getting the better of him, and he didn't mean to take it out on Aurora. *Again.* He took a breath and huffed it out, trying to ease the anger boiling inside of him. He held a hand out to her, to assist her up from the rock.

"Let's just go inside. Please."

Hesitating for a second, she placed her hand in his and allowed him to help her to her feet. Though it was getting dark, they had enough light to have a private conversation.

Once they were inside, the wide-eyed look

of shock on her face gave him pause. He took a deep breath and blew it out before he spoke. Irritated, he ran a hand through his hair and shoved it back from his face. He still hadn't gotten a damned haircut.

"What's wrong? What did I do?" she repeated. Wide-eyed, she faced him.

"Nothing, it was me. I'm sorry I didn't take care of you out there. You're in pain and I didn't realize. I should have had someone relieve you." He strode to her, got as close as he could and placed his hands on her shoulders and squeezed. "Aurora, you're important. You're *very* important. And I don't want you putting yourself in pain unnecessarily."

"Beau."

She tipped her head to look up at him and those dewy blue eyes of hers got to him, stripped him of all propriety and good sense.

"To be perfectly honest I didn't feel anything until I sat in the car to stabilize that kid's neck— then it hit me." She gave a small laugh and patted one hand on his chest, trying to soothe away his irritation. "I think adrenaline gave me such a rush I didn't know it was getting bad 'til then."

"I think it's having the same effect on me, too." In a totally different way.

His concern, masked as anger, dissipated as

he held her close. As he looked down at that tempting mouth of hers. As desire filled him.

"What are you talking about?"

"This."

He pressed his mouth to hers and kissed her. Cupping his hands around her face, he pulled her closer against him and breathed in her scent, touched her skin, eased her in so they were pressed against each other. Tension filled him. This was so good, but so wrong at the same time. He'd leaped over and toppled all the boundaries they'd set.

She was his friend, his employee, and his patient. There were so many reasons he shouldn't be touching her, kissing her, needing her right now. But he ignored all of them as he explored the sweetness of her mouth.

Shaking with need and fear, he pulled back. "I'm sorry, Aurora. I…"

"Shh."

She placed her fingers over his lips and he kissed them. God, she was so beautiful, and so wonderful and he wanted her with everything he had in him. But there were so many reasons not to.

"But—"

"I understand. Completely." Leaning forward, she pressed a small kiss on his mouth, then pulled away. "We have things to do right now—like you going for Chloe, like me getting my pain medicine out and closing up the office for the night." She gave a quick frown. "I may have to stay at my mother's place tonight."

A frown wrinkled his brow at the mention of her pain medicine. "Hold off on the meds for a bit—and your mother. I have a hot tub at my house. Since the office will be closed tomorrow, why don't you come over tonight? We'll put some ice on your back, some heat in the spa, then see if you still need the medication."

"Are you sure?"

"Absolutely."

Relaxing a little, he tried to focus on calming down, on treating Aurora's pain, and controlling the desire thrumming through his system. Months had passed since he'd felt this rampant surge of life rippling through him. The thoughts running through his mind kept telling him no, but the feelings in his heart and his soul told him to let go of the past and move forward. With Aurora.

"I'd like that. I'd like to spend some time with you and Chloe. Just hang out and relax."

"Tonight will be perfect. Just perfect."

Shaking his head, he stepped back and took a breath, not realizing he'd been holding it. Stepping to the now immaculate desk, he found a pen and scribbled on a notepad, then tore the paper off and gave it to Aurora.

"Here's my address. I'll go get Chloe, and grab a pizza from Sanso's Deli. Come over in an hour or so and bring your swimsuit."

"Okay. I'll see you in a bit."

Before Beau could change his mind, or turn around and kiss the daylights out of her, he headed out the door. The parking lot was still torn up, gravel and dirt strewn everywhere. That would have to get taken care of next week. Yet another task that belonged to a small business owner.

At the moment it didn't bother him. What bothered him more was his desire to pull Aurora into his arms and never let go of her.

An hour later, car lights moving across his yard indicated that Aurora had arrived. A flutter of excitement lifted his heart to a faster rate.

Neither of them was ready for a serious relationship, right? Or were they? They were both scared, but one of them had to take the leap of faith.

Chloe squealed in delight at something Daisy had done and it drew his attention. One side of his mouth curved up as he watched his daughter tug on Daisy's ear.

Didn't Chloe deserve a mother? Didn't *he* deserve a wife, a partner and friend? For both of them to love, and hold, and laugh? To live together?

Daisy alerted him to Aurora's presence with her excited romp to the door and a pointed look at him.

"Okay, okay. I'm coming."

That twitch in his pulse returned, and he couldn't prevent the smile on his face. He pulled the door open and the smile on his face froze as he took in Aurora's face. Pale and drawn earlier, her appearance hadn't changed any. She was still in pain.

"Get in here. We've got to get some ice on you right away."

"It's okay. I'm okay."

The stiff movements of her body told him otherwise.

"That's obviously not true." He took the tote bag from her hands. "Sit on the couch beside Chloe and I'll get the ice packs. The pizza can wait."

"Okay." Aurora made her way to the couch and eased onto it.

Babbling and gurgling, Chloe crawled over to Aurora's legs and pulled herself up.

Aurora held her hands out for Chloe to take hold of and she stood on her feet and squealed. "Oh, Beau. Look at this."

He arrived moments later with his hands full of ice packs.

"She's been trying to pull herself up, but hadn't made it that far yet. Pretty soon she'll be walking." Beau sat. "Lean forward." He placed ice packs in strategic areas. "Now lean back."

"Oh, that is *cold*!" She closed her eyes and shivered once. "But I know it's going to ease the burn."

"Yes, it will. We'll hang out here and eat pizza, then get in the tub later."

Beau brought the pizza box over to the coffee table with two bottles of beer.

After sitting for half an hour on the ice, Aurora visibly relaxed. Seeing her hanging out on his couch with his baby on her lap and his dog at her feet tugged at his heart. If things stayed this way, his life would be complete.

This was all he needed—right here in this room.

At that moment he knew he'd fallen for her. The last few weeks had been wonderful, but tonight sealed the deal in his heart.

Chloe had maneuvered herself to face Aurora and now rested her head against Aurora's left arm. The two snuggled together and a soft humming reached his ears.

"That's a beautiful sight." Beau could hardly speak as he watched them together.

"What?"

Aurora looked at him and he felt the full brunt of his emotions in that moment. There were no more questions for him. This was what he needed in his life. Somehow he was going to convince her of it, too.

"The two of you. My beauties." With his right hand, he pushed the hair back over Aurora's shoulder. "Are you okay with her on your lap?"

"Yes." Aurora hugged the little girl against her. "I love having her so close. She's a wonderful baby. You've done such a good job raising her, Beau."

"It's not been easy, and I've had a lot of help." This image of the two of them would remain etched in his mind forever. "I love her so much it hurts, sometimes."

"That's the way it should be, right?"

Unable to stop himself, he leaned closer and pressed his lips against Aurora's for a kiss. "Yes. It should be." He whispered the words from his heart.

After a second's hesitation, she raised her face and parted her lips to his.

The feel of her lips, her tongue against his, was just luscious and it stirred him deeply. "Aurora…"

Chloe took that moment to push at him and he looked down at her.

"Am I squishing you, baby girl?"

He leaned back, but his gaze clung to Aurora's aroused blue gaze. Standing quickly, he took Chloe in his hands and tossed her a few inches into the air. The movement had the desired outcome, and as she squealed with delight the tension between he and Aurora eased.

"I'm ready for the tub now—how about you?"

"Yes."

He tucked Chloe against his side. With the other hand he helped Aurora up from the couch. He led the way down the hall to the guest bathroom.

"You can change in here." He cleared his throat, trying not to imagine her naked and emerging in a tiny red bikini.

Instead, she emerged in an oversized shirt that ended at her knees. "I didn't have a suit, so I figured this would work."

"Absolutely. Can't tell you how disappointed I am, though. I remember that hot red number you used to wear in high school."

"Oh, *you*!" A light blush colored her face, but at least it was some color. "Always the kidder."

"I'm not joking. Not at all."

"Seriously? What's life without a little temptation?" The sparkling light in her eyes caught him off guard.

Timing was everything, and they'd been circling around each other for weeks. Maybe tonight was the night they closed the gap.

"Come this way. You can get soaking, and I'll go change."

He led Aurora to his back patio, where the spa steamed in the evening air.

Aurora stopped, her gaze fastened on the rolling hills of the Appalachian Mountains. "What a stunning view."

"You should see it in October. That's when it's really amazing. The leaves turn incredible colors, and you can sit here and take it all in."

At that, she turned her gaze to him. "I'd... I'd like that Beau. I'd like to sit here...with you... this fall and watch this view."

Intrigued, he moved closer and looked down into her warm and curious eyes. "Then you'll have to stay longer. You'll have to make your time here more than temporary. Are you willing to do that? To give up your life in Virginia? To trade that...for this?"

Leaning in, he pressed another kiss to her mouth.

She gave a nervous lick of her lips and curved her hair around one ear. "I've been thinking about that lately. A lot." After dropping her gaze, she brought it back to his. "And you."

"Well, I think we should talk more about that—but for now, let's get you in."

He took her hand, assisted her over the edge of the padded shelf and waited until she'd swung those long legs into the churning water.

"Oh…" She closed her eyes and squeezed his hand hard. "That's *so* good, Beau. I think I'm in heaven."

Slowly she adjusted to the temperature and eased down onto one of the seats. Another moan of satisfaction escaped her throat as she settled in.

Beau changed into his swim trunks. When he was alone he went naked, but tonight a suit was in order if he intended to maintain his dignity. He dressed Chloe in the suit his mother had bought for her, picked up her floaty ring and settled her against his side, then grabbed two bottles of beer before heading outside.

"Oh, *squee!*" Aurora grinned. "There's the little girl—in a pink swimsuit, too."

Beau made a face. "Grandma thought she needed one—even at this age when she's still wearing a diaper."

"I agree. It's never too early to start having some style."

Chloe squirmed and hooted in delight when she realized where they were going, and Beau nearly lost her, and the beer, but managed to hold on to both.

CHAPTER NINE

"LET ME HELP." Aurora took the bottles from him, and he focused on climbing in with his wiggly daughter safely tucked against him.

"She loves the spa. To her it's a giant bathtub, and we usually have floaty toys swimming around with us." Beau reached into a plastic basket full of toys and tossed a few in, to Chloe's delight.

"I agree with her. This is fabulous." She opened the beer bottles and handed him one. "Thanks. This is really great. I can feel my back relaxing already."

"That's good. Working so physically today— in and out of the car, running in and out of the clinic over a gravel parking lot." He shook his head at his oversight and single-mindedness. "I should have thought of the effect it would have on you. I'm sorry."

"It just reinforces that I'm not cut out for physical work any longer, and it's not your fault.

It's the car crash. Everything comes back to that damned car crash."

She shook her head and a haunted look filled her eyes, as if she were going deep inward, seeing things that he couldn't.

For a few moments they sat in companionable silence, except for the bubbling of the jets and the night birds settling into the trees around the house. Crickets began their nightly song and one lone cicada buzzed from high up in a tree. Chloe slapped the water with her hand and squealed in delight.

"It's so peaceful here. I imagine you just love it." Aurora grabbed one of the toys and sent it over toward Chloe, who splashed in excitement.

"I do. I just...well, it was Julie's dream home."

"Do you want to tell me about her? We're settled in for a soak and a beer. Why not?"

The smile she offered was soothing, compassionate. So very Aurora.

For a nanosecond he *didn't* want to talk about Julie, about his life with her, but here in his arms, squirming and talking nonsense, was the product of his love for Julie. How could he not acknowledge that?

Tree frogs chorused as he gathered his thoughts and absentmindedly he reached for a yellow duck floating just out of arm's reach and handed it to Chloe. She shoved its bill into her mouth and chewed on it.

"Well, the short version is we met in college, fell madly in love, waited until I was out of school to start a family, and when we did she died."

"I'm so sorry, Beau. If it's too painful, I understand."

"I'm okay." He looked at Chloe and determination filled him. He took a deep breath and blew it out, letting go of the pain, of the unfulfilled dreams he'd had. "Some women have bad pregnancies from the beginning, but Julie's was wonderful until she collapsed in her ninth month. The doctors said it was an AVM."

Saying the words out loud still sounded like it had happened to someone else.

"I don't know what that is."

"Arteriovenous malformation. There's a malformation, a growing together, of an artery and a vein in the brain. It usually isn't bothersome until the extra blood supply of a pregnancy puts added pressure on the weak area. And then…" He didn't have to explain.

"Oh, my God." Aurora closed her eyes, anticipation clearly showing on her face. As a nurse, she could follow the implications and come to the correct deadly conclusion.

"As you guessed, it ruptured, and she suffered a catastrophic brain injury. Fortunately we were sitting in the doctor's office when it happened, and she was taken to hospital right away. If it had happened at home I'd have lost them both, and I don't really want to think about that again."

Pulling Chloe closer, he pressed a kiss to her chubby little cheek. Telling the story was difficult, but somehow sharing it with Aurora took some of the sting out of it.

"With Julie's parents, I made the decision to have Chloe delivered by C-section…and then we let her go."

He pressed his lips together as emotions tried to bubble up. The image of removing that life support was something that would never leave him, but now the pain of it wasn't so real.

Without a word, Aurora held her hand out to him. After a second's hesitation he took it, and looked into her watery eyes.

"I'm so sorry, but thank you for telling me. I know it wasn't easy. None of it. But it sounds like you did the right thing—the only thing that could be done."

"Yes. I know. Intellectually, there's no issue. It's just the wondering…if things had gone differently…blah, blah, blah."

"That's always the hardest part, I think. Of

anything. The *what if.* I had the same sort of thoughts about my car crash. If only I'd gone another route that day, would I be fine now?" She met his gaze. "But then I wouldn't be here. With you. And Chloe."

"Yes, well… Grief is something we all go through in life, but that doesn't make it easier. Some days are just fine and other days are not."

Chloe yawned and drew his attention to her sleepy eyes.

"But for now I'd better get this little one out, give her a proper bath, then put her to bed."

"Would it be okay if I stayed in a little while longer? It really is helping." She moved her shoulders back and forth and twisted each one with ease.

"Certainly." He squeezed her hand and released it. "That wasn't a subtle invitation for you to leave."

"If you're sure?" There were questions in her eyes.

"I'm sure."

As he turned away, he didn't know whether he had any answers.

Aurora listened to the sounds of a happy baby splashing in the bathtub and Beau's voice as he played with her. The sounds stirred something

in her heart she'd thought she'd left behind. The
desire for a family of her own. Having been independent and on her own for so many years,
she'd tucked that fantasy away. Now, being with
Beau and Chloe had opened the door to shine
some light on it.

Closing her eyes, she let herself go back, remember. Remember what she'd used to want.
What she'd put aside for her career. Marriage.
Children. A happy home. The warmth in her
heart had nothing to do with the heat of the
water she was simmering in. She raised her
hands.

Definitely pruned. Time to get out of the tub.
Unfortunately Beau wasn't there to offer assistance, and she wasn't willing to risk falling out
of the tub. The rim was too high for her to ease
herself down without jumping. She sat on the
edge, lifting most of her body out and cooling
off, waiting until Beau returned.

In minutes she heard him in the living room
and called out to him. "Beau? Can you help me
get out?"

"Just a minute. I'll put Chloe down."

She heard his footsteps approaching a few
minutes later.

"Okay, you need a—" Beau stopped and
stared at her.

His eyes looked over her body. What she

hadn't counted on, with being covered up by the long shirt, was that it was going to be plastered to her body when she got out.

Beau swallowed and took a step closer to her, his gaze dropping from her face down over her breasts, firmly outlined by the wet shirt. Her nipples stood out prominently and ached to have him touch them. Moments ago she'd been relaxed and lulled by the hot water, but now her breathing came in short, quick gasps, her heart fluttered, and a reckless feeling stirred in her feminine region.

"Beau?"

"Don't move," he whispered, and stepped closer.

He'd changed into a pair of sweat pants and an old shirt, and looked as sexy as she'd ever seen him with his bare feet sticking out. Placing his hands on her knees, he parted them gently and moved between them. "There's no good reason why I should do this, other than I really want to, and many reasons why I shouldn't."

His breathing was as fast as hers, and in the dim light she could see the desire filling his face, in his posture, in everything.

"Do what?" she dared to ask. She wanted to know. *Now.*

"This." He leaned over, took one of her nipples in his mouth and sucked.

Aurora gasped at the sensation of his hot mouth closing over her chilled, taut flesh. She clutched his shoulders and hung on.

"Oh!"

Beau's tongue and mouth caressed and tortured her nipple, stirring feelings she'd thought were long gone. Now she realized they'd only been dormant, waiting for the right moment to surface. Tenderly, he slid his arms around her, moved to her other nipple and closed his mouth over it, tearing down any resistance she might have thought of.

Neither of them had been prepared for a relationship—hadn't thought of it until circumstances had brought them together. Now she knew this was what she wanted, and it seemed like Tammie was right. The universe had led her here…right into his arms.

A soft moan escaped Aurora's throat as he stirred her body to perfection. Moving upward, spreading kisses, Beau reached her mouth. He cupped her head in his hands and kissed her thoroughly, parting her lips and taking her deep as his tongue sought hers. This was so wonderful—to be wanted, and kissed, and touched, and held in Beau's arms.

He pulled back and rested his forehead against hers, his rapid breath matching hers. "Aurora,

I want so badly to take you to bed right now, but if it's too soon, and you're not ready, or—"

"I'm ready."

The words sprang out of her mouth, but emerged from her soul. This was the moment she'd been waiting for and hadn't even known it.

"I'm ready." With hands that trembled, she cupped his head in her hands. "Kiss me again."

With those words, Beau groaned and complied, teasing her lips with his, rubbing his nose against hers, then parting her lips with his tongue. The night creatures around them lent a natural music that stirred her desire to be with Beau—now. Everything was perfect.

He pulled back and looked down at her body. He frowned.

"What?" She looked down and couldn't see anything wrong.

"You simply can't wear that shirt inside. It's all wet. And dripping."

"I see." Aurora liked this sexy, playful side of Beau. "What do you suppose we should do about that?"

"It needs to go, for sure."

He clasped the hem of it, which was hanging around her knees, and pulled it up over her head. She shivered once, the cool air chilling her, raising goosebumps on her skin. It was a strange sensation, having the air teasing her body and Beau's gaze stirring it further.

"I think we'd better get you inside and dried off."

"If you'll help me get down from here."

A zing of fear hit her. How would he react to her scars? The pulse pounded in her throat and she swallowed. There was only one way to know—one way to move forward. If they were going to have any chance at a relationship she had to bare herself to him, scars and all.

"I can arrange something."

He returned to his former position between her knees and clasped her hips, bringing them against his. He lifted her against him and let her slide down the length of his body. The soft cloth of his sweats didn't hide the hard arousal within. She ached to touch him, to feel his skin sliding against hers and join their bodies together.

Once they entered the house and closed the door to the patio everything changed. The intensity of Beau was almost overwhelming as his hands clasped her by the hips and brought her against him.

Any sane thought went out the window as Aurora allowed herself to breathe in his scent, to savor the sensations he created in her, knowing he was feeling the same.

"This is so good...so wonderful to touch you,

to have you against me." Aurora tunneled her hands beneath his shirt and drew it upward.

He flung it to the floor. "I just don't want to hurt you."

That made her pull back a little from him to look into green eyes that were filled with need for her. "Hurt me?"

"Your back." He stroked her face and pressed a kiss to her nose, breathed in her scent again.

"I have an idea about that," she said. "Why don't you lead the way?"

She grabbed her purse from the kitchen counter and followed him. In just a few seconds they entered his bedroom, and he led her to a large four-poster. The sheets were warm against her skin, and together they tangled themselves up in the covers and each other.

Aurora leaned into Beau, and then lay him back, draped over the top of his chest. "This is my idea…"

"I see."

Kisses and breaths mingled as they learned each other's bodies for the first time. A stroke here, a lingering kiss there, licking, sucking, touching, tasting, all bringing them closer to each other.

Aurora was ready, and moisture filled her feminine sheath. She tugged on his pants and he swiftly removed them, leaving nothing but skin between them.

"Lie back," she said, and moved over on top of him, straddling his hips. She clutched his erection in her hand and feminine power pulsed deep within her. This was the moment she'd been waiting for.

"I don't have a—"

"I do."

"Really?" Beau's eyebrows twitched upward and a Cheshire cat smile covered his face.

"Really."

She dug a condom from her purse and tore the cellophane package open with her teeth. Keeping her eyes on his, she removed the condom, then slid it down over his erection. Watching his eyes close at the pleasure of her touch thrilled her. This was so beautiful. So *right*.

Rising up further on her knees, she lowered herself onto him. Though she hadn't made love in a long time, her body was ready. As they joined together for the first time new and beautiful sensations overwhelmed her as her body accommodated his.

"Oh..." A moan stirred from her throat as she took him in all the way.

Beau's hands clasped her hips and he began to rock her in rhythm to the movements of his own hips. "You feel incredible, Aurora. *Incred-*

ible." One hand strayed upward to caress her breast and stir her nipple.

Drawing herself upright, she placed her hands beside his knees and allowed herself to take in sensation after sensation, to feel the power of him inside her, to be a woman fully for the first time in way too long.

Beau slid his hands up her thighs, his fingers lightly grazing her skin and sending a thrill through her. He delved one thumb into her folds, searching for the center of her pleasure zone, and teased it softly.

Her breath caught in her throat as his hips, his touch, his body sent her over the edge and she shattered, clutching the bedding in her hands and crying out her pleasure. Wave after wave pulsed through her.

Sensing a change in Beau's breathing, she lifted her head and focused on him. She moved his hands to her hips to help her keep the pace that would satisfy him, bring him to his peak. Digging his fingers into her hips he rocked her and plunged into her sheath. Faster and harder. Then he clutched her tightly as he found his release.

She draped her torso forward, allowing her chest to touch his, then released her weight with a sigh.

"This was beautiful, Beau."

* * *

"Absolutely."

Her words and the sound of her voice drew him in and pushed him away at the same time. Being with another woman, loving another woman, was hard. He'd never dreamed life would turn out this way. He'd never dreamed he'd lose himself in the arms of a woman again and that that woman would be Aurora.

"Where are you?" she asked, drawing his attention to her mouth again.

"Lost in space, I guess."

She placed a hand on his face and moved in for a long, slow kiss. "What are we going to do about this, Beau?"

"About what? Us?" He eased his hands up her back, drawing his hands across her smooth, silky skin until an irregularity stopped him. "What's this?"

"A scar. I had a chest tube for a few days after the crash. It's ugly. Don't look at it."

"It saved your life." Just as she was saving *his* right now. "About your question… I don't know what we're going to do. I just know I don't want you to leave."

That made her drop her gaze away from his again. "Do you mean tonight, or what?"

"I mean I don't want you to leave Brush Valley." With one hand, he curved her hair behind her ear and cupped her face. "It's only been a few weeks, but we've connected in a way I never imagined, and I don't want to let go of that any time soon."

"Me, either. It's too soon for either of us to be making promises, though, don't you think?" Closing her eyes for a second, she savored the sensation of his hand, warm against her face.

"I know. I don't want either of us to make any promises we can't keep or will feel guilty about if things change." He raised his face to hers and encouraged her to press another kiss to his lips. "I want a chance with you, Aurora. That's all. I just want to give *us* a chance. Be my partner, be a mother to Chloe? Are you willing to do that? Are you willing to stay, to work with me in the office and see if we can make it work?"

The intensity of him was overwhelming. "I know we can make it work in the office. It's the other stuff, the personal stuff, I'm not sure about."

"Is it because of Chloe?"

He had to ask. Not every woman was prepared to take on a child *and* a new relationship.

The shock on her face was his answer.

"*No!* Absolutely not. She's a delight, and I would be happy to be part of her life." She sighed and pulled away, then sat up on the edge of the bed. "But what if *we* don't work out? It's not fair to Chloe to think I'm going to be around and then for me not to be here."

"There are no guarantees in life." He snorted out a bitter laugh. "*My* life is certainly evidence of that."

"I'm not asking for a guarantee, Beau."

"Yes, you are. You aren't saying it in so many words, but that's what it is—and I don't know. I just don't know." He tugged on his sweats and a shirt while she wrapped the sheet around herself. "This is not the conversation I envisioned us having after making love the first time."

"Me, either." One side of her mouth lifted in a half-hearted smile. "How about we go back a few minutes and agree to see how things go? I'd like that."

She moved closer to him and placed a hand on his chest. The heat of it moved through him, warming his heart.

"I'd like that, too."

Wrapping his arms around her shoulders, he brought her up against him for a few minutes and just held on as emotions threatened to swamp him.

What if she was right? What if their relationship didn't work out? Then what? Was it really fair to Chloe to present her with a new mother, then watch her walk away?

* * *

The next day dawned bright and shiny. Aurora was slow to get moving, enjoying the peace of the quiet morning, the chirping of birds in the field beside the office as they foraged for seeds and insects trapped by the morning dew.

She turned on the light switch, but nothing happened. The power was still out.

Though Beau had asked her to stay the night with him, she'd declined. She wasn't ready for that yet, and she didn't think he was either. It was too much, too fast. Making love had been wonderful, but now she wondered if that had been a mistake, too.

Were they just two lonely, damaged people who'd sought a moment of comfort in each other's arms? It had been known to happen. Were they really a relationship in the making?

Her phone rang, ending her peaceful moment.

"Hello?"

"It's your mother."

"Hi, Mom. What's up? Everything okay?"

"Sure. Can't I call my daughter without there being a crisis?"

Aurora wondered, and suppressed a snort of amusement. "Well, when I was living in Virginia you only called when someone died or there was a disaster."

"Yes, well, today's different. I wanted to see if

you wanted to go to Smicksburg with me today."
There was hope and eagerness in her mother's
voice. "If you don't have anything else planned,
I mean."

"No. I don't have any plans."

Nothing that couldn't wait anyway, like laundry and bills. With no power in the apartment,
she wasn't going to do much else. "Sounds like
fun."

"Good. I'll pick you up in thirty minutes,
then."

"Make it an hour. I'm just waking up." She
needed to do her exercises and get something
to eat.

"Oh, I suppose... I'll pack us some lunch and
it'll be a fun day."

"Great. See you soon."

Aurora threw the covers off and got moving.
As she packed her purse with necessary supplies she hesitated over whether to take her pain
medications with her, but she grabbed the bottle
and tossed them in. She locked up and waited
for her mother in front of the building.

The parking lot had been really torn up by the
car crash last evening. It was definitely going
to need some professional work done, not just
a few shovels full of dirt.

Pulling out her phone, she made a call to a

friend to see if he could help out. Just as she finished the call she spied her mother's little SUV.

"Thanks, Tim. I'll talk to you later."

"Right on time," her mother said as she got into the car. "I don't like to wait on anyone, you know."

"I know. So let's get going and have a great day."

This could be an opportunity to repair her relationship with her mother, which had always been a bit tense.

"Who were you talking to?"

"Tim. An old high school buddy. I wanted to see if he could bring his grader and smooth out the parking lot for Beau."

"He's the owner. Shouldn't *he* be doing that?"

"Oh, sure he could, but as his office nurse I can make a call and get it done for him. He's got Chloe all day today, and if I can take one thing off his plate then I'm happy to do it."

"You *are*?" Sally nodded.

"What's that supposed to mean?" Aurora cast a suspicious glance at her mother.

"Nothing." There was an upward inflection to her voice, solidifying Aurora's suspicions.

"Mom, with you there's never 'nothing.'" There was always something behind any comment her mother made.

"Oh, I was just thinking that since you're

so involved in the office, and Beau, you might think about staying for a while." The last sentence was all said in a rush.

This was it. *This* was the reason for the "spontaneous" trip. Even though Aurora had promised to go on a day trip with her mother, there was definitely a mission behind this one today. Her mother was pumping her for information.

Before answering, Aurora took a breath and centered herself, as she'd learned to do in rehab. "It's hard to say at this point, Mom." Facts—just facts at this point. "Beau has a nurse who has simply gone on maternity leave. We don't know if she's coming back or not."

"Doesn't he have room for more than one nurse? Seems like business is booming."

"At this point, no—but that could change in the future."

"Every time I drive by someone's always coming in or going out. So it's getting busier, right? That's good."

"Yes, it is getting busier, and we have some plans for promotion—like at Brush Valley Day and at the fair."

"Wonderful. Maybe there will be enough business to keep you here full-time, then."

"That's a whole lot of speculation right now. For today, how about we just forget about work, plans, the future, and just have a nice day together? The leaves will be starting to turn, so we'll have to plan another trip for that, too."

After a moment's hesitation her mother agreed. Though Aurora sensed her mother wanted to push her point and drag this conversation on.

"Okay," she said finally. "Today is just about us having a good time." She cast a quick sideways glance at Aurora. "And eating. We can't forget that part."

A warmth filled her chest, and Aurora laughed. Maybe there was hope for healing the relationship with her mother after all. "Definitely not—especially if you're the one who's cooking."

They spent the day together, wandering through the Amish village, shopping, talking and thoroughly enjoying themselves. But with all the walking, getting in and out of the SUV, the bumpy roads and sitting for too long, Aurora's pain soon sprang up from her hips, spreading like wildfire through a dry forest with nothing to stop it.

By the time her mother dropped her at the office seven hours later she didn't think she would be able to make it up the stairs. Though she'd taken one of her pain medications an hour ago, it hadn't helped.

Dammit. Things had been going so well. Until now.

With hands that trembled, she called Beau.

"Aurora?"

The sound of his voice saying her name in her ear was immediately reassuring. He would help her. No matter what happened between them, she knew she could count on him.

"Beau." Tears filled her eyes as she let herself go, let herself need someone—need Beau. "I need you. Can you meet me at the office?"

"Yes. What's wrong? Are you okay?"

There was immediate focus in his voice, which reassured her further.

"I need you to come as soon as you can."

In the background she heard rustling, and Chloe's happy baby sounds. Though she hated to disturb him, there was no help for it. She couldn't drive to meet him.

"I'll be there in fifteen minutes. Hang on, darling. I'll be there. Don't worry."

"Thank you," she whispered into the disconnected line.

She unlocked the office, dropped her purse and the bags with her purchases just inside the door. She flipped on the light switch and the lights responded. Power had been restored while she was gone.

Within fifteen minutes she heard the crunching of tires on the gravel and knew relief was just moments away. The door opened and Daisy bounded in, rushing over to greet her, then Beau, looking casual and handsome with his arms full of baby girl. The concern on his face made her wish she hadn't put it there.

CHAPTER TEN

"I KNOW YOU'RE in pain. What happened?"

He set Chloe's bouncy chair on the floor and placed her in it. Though he paid attention to what he was doing, he spoke to Aurora. When Chloe was strapped in, he turned to her, and his expression changed from concern to empathy as he read her posture and her face. He knew. He knew just what she needed.

Opening his arms wide, he walked toward her and placed those strong arms around her, holding her for just a moment.

The tears she'd been holding back could no longer be contained. This was where she needed to be—here, in this man's arms. "I'm so sorry to drag you to the office on a Saturday, but my back is on fire."

"You were fine last night." He pulled back to look at her face and used his thumbs to wipe away the trails of tears on her cheeks. "What did you do? Go rock climbing today or something?"

That made her laugh, and a smile won its way onto her face. "No. I took a long car ride with Mom to Smicksburg, walked all over creation, up and down stairs, in and out of the car. Now I'm paying the price. I don't think I can even get upstairs to the apartment right now."

He glanced down at his daughter, happily bouncing in her chair, trying to make her way toward Daisy. "She'll be okay for a while. How about I see what I can do to get you straightened out again?"

"Thanks, Beau. I knew I could count on you."

"Always, sweet. *Always.*"

Thirty minutes later Beau had massaged and made several adjustments to Aurora's back and the relief was significant.

"I think this is a reminder for you to be more careful, and that you're not ready to go gallivanting across the country—even if it is with your mother."

"You mean it's a *lesson.*"

It felt akin to being sent to the principal's office, but that ended when Beau placed a finger under her chin and raised her face to his.

"No, I don't like that term. Too punitive. An 'opportunity for growth'—that's what I like to call these little life experiences." His brows twitched at that.

"You're kidding, right?"

"No, I'm not. I've been through enough pain to last me the rest of my life. I'm not giving in to it. I'm not letting it get me. I am just acknowledging I may have to adjust my game plan now and then."

"You're so positive, Beau! How can you be positive after the devastating blows life has handed you?"

"It ain't easy, my sweet." He stepped a little closer to her and drew her against his chest, holding her as if she were a fragile thing. "But if life hadn't delivered those blows I wouldn't be holding you in my arms right now, would I? The same is true for you. Maybe we had to go through the tough times alone in order to find each other now."

That silenced her. The pain of it. The truth of it. Without the car crash and ensuing difficulties she wouldn't be here right now with him, falling in love with him in a way she'd never thought possible. And she *was* falling for him— she couldn't deny it.

"How are we going to deal with this? I mean—"

"I know you're a planner. Every nurse I know is. But right now there's no plan, no schedule of events. We live in the moment."

"Then—"

"We just see. We wait, see how things go, and

in the meantime we enjoy ourselves." He kissed her temple, then her cheek, his breath warm on her skin. "Thoroughly."

Warmth spread from her lower abdomen outward and settled in her chest. Never mind falling—she was so in love with Beau already. When he said stuff like that to her it didn't help her resolve not to give in to the feelings in her heart.

"I see." A frown crossed her face as she remembered something she'd been going to do tonight. "Rats. I was going to take Tammie's yoga class this evening, but I don't think I could drive to town."

"How about I drive you? Chloe and I can hang around while you stretch. Then I can ice it afterward."

"Again with the ice?" A smile tried to work its way across her face and her heart lightened a bit. Spending time with Beau and Chloe was never a bad time.

"No hot tub for you tonight."

"I'm not getting into a giant bowl of ice water either." That was *not* happening.

A chuckle escaped his throat. "No. Just ice packs will be fine."

"Okay, then. I accept your offer to drive me to class." Another thought occurred to her. "People will see us going in together and make assumptions. Are you ready for that?"

In small towns like this, any sort of activity—no matter how innocent—was subject to speculation and gossip. Stopping the fire after it was a raging inferno was impossible.

"I'm good." He nodded and seemed not bothered. "I know the truth. So do you. That's all that's important—if *you're* okay with being seen with us."

A slight frown crossed his face. She almost didn't see it, but it was evident he did have some concerns, too.

"Oh, absolutely! I didn't mean to imply anything like that." She placed a hand on his arm, offering him reassurance. "I just wanted to give you the opt-out in case you were...you know, bugged by it."

"Hardly."

Unhappy baby squeals caught their attention.

"Let's go see what kind of mischief the little miss has gotten herself into."

They entered the waiting room and found Chloe had bounced herself into a corner. After scooping her up and planting sloppy kisses on her neck, making her squeal in delight, Beau tucked her against his side, ushered Daisy out and locked the office behind them.

Then he stopped dead in his tracks, his mouth

hanging open, shock etched on his face. He looked at Aurora.

"What happened out here?"

"What do you mean? It looks fine to me." Aurora looked around at the parking lot. The perfectly groomed parking lot that only hours before had been torn up from one end to the other.

"The gravel. It's all where it's supposed to be."

"Oh! I almost forgot. I called Tim Verner to see if he could bring one of his graders and go over the lot. I hope that was okay?" She chewed her lower lip, hesitating. Had she overstepped her boundaries as the office nurse?

Beau looked at her and shook his head. *Okay?* Are you kidding me? It's *fabulous*! Just look at this place. It looks better than new."

The warmth that had been circulating in her chest pulsed hot and deep within her. Pleasure and joy at his response thrilled her. "Oh, good."

"There's only one problem I can see right now."

His eyes widened, and he gave her a look she wasn't able to quite figure out.

"What's that?" Everything looked fine to her.

"I'm probably going to be doing free back adjustments for Verner for the next year to make up for it."

"He wouldn't do that, would he?" She hadn't thought of that.

"No, I'm teasing." He finished buckling Chloe into her seat then turned to Aurora. "I probably shouldn't do that, but it's so much fun to see that pink color in your face. Reminds me of the old days, when anything I said to you made you blush."

"Just *stop*, you."

She gave a playful push against his arm, but he caught her hand before she could pull it away. He reeled her in and brought her close against him.

"Never." His eyes darkened as he looked down at her mouth, seconds before he pressed his lips to hers.

Heart fluttering, Aurora lifted her face to his and reveled in the simplicity of the kiss and felt herself falling over the edge of that cliff she'd sworn never to approach again with such careless abandon as she had in the past. Here she was, teetering on the edge, and no longer caring if she fell as long as she was falling into Beau's arms.

"Let's get you to class, so you're not late." Beau squeezed her arms and pulled away.

"It's okay. It's Tammie teaching it. She won't get upset."

"In my experience I've learned it's best never

to annoy a redheaded woman. Knowing Tammie as well as I do, I think it's doubly important."

"Good point. Let's go."

After a short ride to the community center, they walked in together to the great room where many activities took place. Several people acknowledged them, and she recognized others she hadn't seen for years. From school, from church, and from various other times in her life.

Turning back to Beau, she gave a nod, choking back the sudden nameless emotion trying to squeeze her throat shut. "See you after the class."

"Okay. Have fun—just don't overdo it."

"I won't." She watched as he took Chloe into the children's playroom and closed the door, then grabbed a yoga mat and joined the others.

"Nice to see you could make it, Aurora." Tammie was sitting on a mat at the front of a class of about ten ladies of varying ages.

"Yes. Sorry I'm a few minutes late, but I needed a lift."

"Hmm… Yes…" Tammie nodded at where Beau could be seen through the window of the children's room. "A handsome man always gives *me* a lift, too."

She winked as the other women chuckled at her small joke.

"Okay. Let's take a deep breath in and blow it out, then another one…and hold."

Once the class began in earnest Aurora focused, tried to follow the instructions and let the soothing sound of her friend's voice help her let go of the tension and the knots in her back.

Beau's words about living in the moment helped, and she pushed away all the stress of the day and the last few months with each breath she took.

Beau watched, trying not to look like he was watching, as the class moved through varying positions. He tried to tell himself he was just keeping an eye on Aurora. He was concerned about her back, about her safety. Watching her was only reassuring him that she was okay, given the condition she had been in earlier today.

Yeah, right.

His tongue was all but hanging out and it was all he could do not to stare. Hard.

The sight of her stretching, the moves she made and the focus on her face took his feelings for her to a new level. Well beyond what he'd thought he'd feel again for a woman. The new pulse in his chest, the recent smile on his face and, frankly, the aching throb in his groin. All new. All wonderful. All because of Aurora.

He was living again.

This was what they could be doing every week—working in their community and being a family. Together. Though guilt still took refuge in his heart, its stronghold had been breached since Aurora had landed in his life. Again.

Chloe stood on her feet, balancing against a little table, and squealed at him, then took a few stumbling steps toward him.

"You're trying to walk, baby?"

A grin shot across his face and his heart thrummed as he watched his baby girl try to take her first step. All wobbly legs and flailing arms, she hooted with excitement.

"I wish Aurora could see you right now."

A cramp in his heart killed the smile.

I wish Julie could see you right now.

His phone rang, jerking him out of his musings, and his heart almost stopped as he read the number.

"Hello, Darlene."

He closed his eyes, bracing himself to talk to his mother-in-law. The sound of her voice was so close to Julie's that he'd had a difficult time talking to her in the days after Julie's death. Each time she called it got easier, but right now it was like some demon had dragged him back in time.

"Beau. Sorry to bother you, but I was wondering when you could bring Chloe over for a visit. We haven't seen her for a few weeks, and I miss that little darling."

"Of course. You know you can see her any time."

They made arrangements for the following afternoon, for Chloe to spend several hours with her grandparents. He wanted her to know them, and know her mother through them, though it was still hard for all of them.

Puzzled at the bitter feelings suddenly swirling inside him, he took a breath and blew it out, like Tammie was teaching in the class. Maybe he should sign up for one, too.

Minutes later the ladies rose from their mats, bundled them up and left the room. He gathered Chloe and met Aurora in the great room again, well aware that a number of people observed his actions.

"How was it?" he asked Aurora as she approached.

"Wonderful. Thanks for—"

Chloe interrupted by leaning toward Aurora and holding her arms out.

"Looks like she wants to go to you." Beau adjusted his position, to pull her back, but she insisted, crying out and wiggling to get her way.

"Oh!" Aurora held her hands out to the baby. "You want to come have a visit with me, do you?" Chloe rewarded her with a delighted squeal. "Well, there's a happy girl now."

"Indeed." Beau released Chloe to Aurora's arms and for the first time in months felt the release of the strain of being a single parent. "Looks good on you."

"Yes... What?" Aurora's eyes popped wide, and she gaped at Beau.

"You look like you should have a baby in your arms." He shrugged and she closed her mouth. "I'm just saying you look comfortable with her, and she likes you. She doesn't ask just *anyone* to hold her."

"I see that." Aurora adjusted the baby more comfortably on her hip as they left the building, knowing full well they were being watched.

"Does it bother you?"

"A little." After they'd left the building she looked up at him. "I'm finding I'm less bothered than I thought."

"Good. Then it's okay if I do this." Before he thought better of it he leaned over and kissed her on the mouth, leisurely, exploring her mouth, until Chloe had had enough and bashed him in the nose with her fist.

"What was that for?" Aurora asked, her eyes soft and searching his for answers.

"Because you're wonderful, and I thought you should know it."

He cleared his throat. Was this the right time to say it? Was this the right time to say *anything*? What about his desire to live in the moment, not to plan too far ahead? Out the window when he kissed her.

"Oh. Thanks. You're wonderful, too."

Beau finally got a clue as he watched her reposition the baby again. "Here. Let me take her. Holding her is not good for your back."

He took Chloe from Aurora's arms and tossed her a little into the air, eliciting an excited scream from her.

"Beau, be careful."

"It's okay. I'm not going to drop her." He tucked Chloe against his side and then pulled Aurora close to his other side.

This is the way it's supposed to be, he thought. *This is what I want, and somehow, some way, I need to help Aurora see it, too.*

The last few weeks before Brush Valley Day had been a bustle of activity. Though she and Beau had spent a lot of time together at the office, their private time together had been limited. Neither one of them had pushed to repeat the intimacy of their one night together, sensing the need each of them had for space, time to think and make decisions. Beau had said to see how things went and they were. Cautiously.

As Aurora left her apartment the day before Brush Valley Day a hint of crisp fall air teased her face and tugged a strand of hair across her face. Fall was her favorite time of the year. Summers in Pennsylvania were hot and muggy, winters were too cold, and her feet didn't thaw out until spring.

Fall was peace. It made sense. The energy in the air was filled with comfort. Things were the way they were supposed to be. The intense energy and flurry of summer wound down. Leaves turned vibrant, earthy tones in this valley in the heart of the Appalachian Mountain range. No matter where she turned, beauty surrounded her.

Standing for a few moments on the stairs, she looked around, taking in the staggering beauty of the early morning. She stood there and looked at the rolling hills surrounding her. A dark-winged crow warbled a morning greeting to her. Overhead, a flock of geese in classic V formation made their way from their northern summer climes to their wintering grounds far to the south.

A hint of tears filled her eyes as the beauty of nature surrounded her, filling her with a bittersweet pain. She could take in this scene every day if she chose to. All she had to do was reach out to Beau, let go of her past, and take his hand to build a new future with him.

She snorted. That was *all*?

Carrying on with her morning duties as she did every day, Aurora opened the door, turned on the lights, cranked up the cooling system and fired up the coffee pot. She'd have to talk to Beau about offering coffee to patients and their families, hot chocolate for the kids, when the practice got busier.

Just as she was going through the mail from yesterday, she stopped.

Was she planning on being there when things got busier? That thought paused her heart for a few seconds. She hadn't planned on it originally. Now…?

She could easily envision herself working with Beau, helping to grow the practice, spending weekends with him and Chloe, watching her grow too.

Tears filled her eyes at the thought that everything she'd ever wanted was within her reach. A relationship. A marriage. A family. All of it. Right there.

Dismissing her tears, and her thoughts of a fantasy long past, she took a breath and tried to put it aside.

It's only fall that's making me this way. It's the change of seasons. Always gets to me.

Reaching for her notebook, which was getting fuller every day, she wrote it down. Maybe Cathy would want to institute having refreshments when she came back. Her maternity leave was going to be ending soon. Aurora added that to her list of things to do. Call Cathy to see when she was going to return to work.

Call Cathy to see when Aurora's life was going to change again. Call Cathy to see when she had to move, find a new job, leave everything she'd grown to love.

The tears she'd thought she'd set aside managed to push themselves to the front again, insistent that she deal with them. Right now.

As she sat down the unmistakable click of Daisy's nails neared the desk. Her insides began to tremble, feeling the excitement of seeing Beau first thing every morning.

The phone rang, and out of reflex training Aurora answered it. "Brush Valley Medical Clinic. May I help you?"

Lunch arrived with a new patient, just before they were ready to take a break.

"Can I help you?" Aurora looked up, then grinned. "Wait. I know you, don't I?"

The man's face was familiar, but at the same time not. Narrowing her eyes, she studied him.

"You sure do, if you're Aurora Hunt."

The man was about her age, and had a few sun-kissed wrinkles on his face. He was dressed in work jeans and dirty work boots, looking like he'd just come in from a barn. He removed the cowboy hat and peered closer at her.

"Recognize the eyes?"

"Tim?" Aurora moved out from behind the desk. "Tim Verner, you ole cowboy. Thank you so much for sorting the car park. How the heck *are* you?"

She hugged the man who had gone to school with her and Beau.

"I've had better days." He gave her a one-armed hug that was halfhearted at best. Not like his usual boisterous self that she remembered.

"Is that what brings you in?" She indicated his dangling left arm.

"I tripped on a stray board and fell over."

"What did you hit?"

Knowing him, it could be anything from a stack of hay to an old engine hanging from the ceiling in his barn.

"Actually, I caught myself, but when I stood up again I had this going on." He raised his left hand for her to see and there was a rusty nail sticking out of it.

"Geez. *Tim!*" She took hold of his wrist and held it out away from her, like it was a dead rat. "Why didn't you say so in the first place?"

She drew him toward the back. There was no time to waste in this situation. If they didn't act now he could die from infection, tetanus, or even lose the hand.

"Beau! I need you—*now*!"

"That's what I like to hear." Beau put a smile on his face to greet his patient, but when he saw Aurora holding Tim's arm up he froze for a second, then shot into emergency mode. "Holy hell, Tim!"

"That's what I said, too." Tim cleared his throat. "Among other things."

"Get in here." Beau directed him to the first patient room. "Aurora, get the hand trauma kit. It's in the cupboard over the sink."

"We *have* a hand trauma kit?" she asked, confused but impressed by his thinking.

"We do. Brush Valley is an agricultural community. From the day I opened the doors a farmer has come in every week with some sort of hand injury. I just came up with a kit to make it easy."

"Got it." She dashed out and returned in a few seconds with the appropriate item.

"Got any whiskey in there?" Tim asked with hope in his eyes. "Hurts like hell."

For the first time, Aurora noticed that under that farmer's tan of his he was pale.

"Sorry. Not a good idea now." Beau shook

his head as he opened the tray and removed the sterile coverings.

"I know—but *damn*." He shook his head and clenched his teeth.

"Let me get a look at it first. Then I can give you something for the pain."

Tim nodded and clenched his teeth.

Beau put on a pair of specialty magnifying glasses in order to see deeply into the wound, then peeled back the dirty and bloody handkerchief wrapped around the hand.

"How did you do this?" Beau asked without looking up.

"Tripped. Caught myself on an old board with a rusty nail sticking out of it."

"When was your last tetanus shot?" Aurora asked.

"Hell if I know. I know you're supposed to get them boosters every couple years or so, right?" He looked to Aurora for clarification.

"Ten years, but every five if someone has increased risk. Like you." She raised a brow at him, letting him know he was one of *those* people.

"I guess…" He looked away.

"Don't worry, Tim, you're not the only one around town who's not caught up on his shots." She looked at Beau. "Ooh. I just thought of something. Maybe we can add that to our roster at Brush Valley Day."

"What?"

"Seeing if people are up to date on their shots, like tetanus. Adults need shots too—not just babies. In addition to the flu shots and pneumonia. *Oh!* We're going to have to order more serum."

"Good idea. Put it on the list." He sounded distracted as he focused on the injury. "I'm going to need some Lidocaine and a twenty-two gauge needle."

"Needle? What for?" Tim's jaw dropped a second. "A needle? *Really?*"

"I have to pull the nail out and it's gonna hurt, so I want to numb the area."

"No. Just yank it outta there." Tim reached for the nail.

"No!" Aurora and Beau yelled at the same time.

Tim paused. "Why not? Can't hurt any worse coming out than it did going in."

"We don't want to damage any more flesh, nerves or tendons. It has to be done carefully. Ideally by a hand surgeon."

"I see."

"I'll get the Lido." Aurora left the room, and Beau watched her go.

"She gonna stay this time?" Tim asked.

"What?" Beau was having a hard time shifting gears today.

"Aurora. She gonna stay this time around? Seems like she needs a place to stay put instead of living down there in Virginia. She say anything about whether she's gonna stay?"

"She's just helping me while my nurse is out on maternity leave." Beau pressed his lips together as he said the words. Still not liking the idea.

"You should try to get her to stay. We can use good people like her around here."

"That's exactly what I thought," Beau said aloud, and looked over the glasses at Tim. A snort escaped Beau's nose before he could stop it. "Exactly what I *told* her, too."

"Thought what and told who what?" Aurora asked as she returned to the room.

"Nothing…" Beau and Tim chorused at the same time, trying very hard to not look guilty.

Aurora snorted and gave them both the stink eye, the way she had back in high school. "Like I'm gonna believe *that* anytime soon."

She handed a syringe to Beau.

"Here's the Lido. I'll go round up some tetanus booster."

"Oh, man," Tim said, concern in his eyes and a frown on his brow.

"What?" she asked, and gave Tim a look.

It was all Beau could do not to laugh at the look on Tim's face. He looked like he was heading to the executioner.

"Am I gonna have to drop my drawers for that one?"

"Only if you really want to, Tim. But I'd rather not be traumatized. I can give it in your arm."

Without another word she left the room.

CHAPTER ELEVEN

TIM GRINNED AT BEAU. "Feisty now, isn't she?"

"You have *no* idea."

Tim eased forward a little bit, his bright blue eyes eager for some gossip. "Tell me. I'm gonna be here a while, so tell me."

"No way, Tim." Beau reached for sterile saline to cleanse the wound and distract Tim from the direction he wanted to take the conversation. "This might hurt."

"Oh—*oh!*" Tim sat straight up and hissed a breath out between clenched teeth.

Aurora returned and rolled up Tim's sleeve. "Hold still." She jabbed the needle into his arm and injected tetanus vaccine while he was occupied with Beau.

"Damn, you two. You're double-teaming me."

"It's easier that way." Aurora rubbed the injection site on Tim's arm. "It'll be sore for a few days, but after that you'll be good as new."

"Dangit. Now *both* arms hurt."

"Tim." Beau looked at the man and removed the specialty glasses. "I'm going to have to send you to the ER after all. This is beyond me. I don't want to take a chance on damaging anything."

"No," Tim said and shook his head adamantly, his eyes no longer glittering with amusement. "I'm not going to town for this. If you can't do it I'll do it myself."

Before Aurora or Beau could react Tim had grabbed the nail and yanked it out of his hand.

"Holy hell, that hurts!" he said, and dropped the nail. His face was three shades of pale and he looked like he was going to faint.

Aurora and Beau jumped into action and pressed sterile gauze to the gaping hole in the middle of his hand. But there was little blood.

"Let me see what you've done this time." Beau put the glasses on again. "I'll be damned..." Beau said, and eased the gauze back from Tim's hand. "Only you, Tim. Only *you* could do this."

"What'd I do now?"

"Only you can trip over your own feet, fall on a nail and miss every vessel and tendon in your hand." He shook his head.

"I did? Then why's it still hurting so much?"

"You still have a hole in your hand. With a few stitches and a visit to a hand doctor you'll be in good shape in a few weeks."

"Weeks?" Tim shook his head again. "No way. I gotta be back on the job in an hour. Keith dropped me off and went to get us some lunch at Greg's Diner. He'll be back in an hour."

"You're going to have to knock off for the day. Sorry."

"Nope. Ain't gonna do it. Just wrap it up." He pressed his lips firmly together.

"Tim, don't be a horse's—" Beau started, but was interrupted by Aurora.

"Let me interject a little sanity, a little perspective, into your life here, Tim."

Calm as Beau had ever seen her, Aurora placed a hand on Tim's shoulder and gave him a smile that he'd bet she'd often turned on doctors and medical students who were just about to do something monumentally stupid.

"Go for it."

This he had to see. Beau sat back and gave her the floor.

"You have a lot of people who depend on you, right?"

"See? You *do* understand. That's why I need to get back to work."

"So, I just have one question for you. What if your hand gets infected, rots and falls off? Your family—the people who depend on you—will not be happy when your business falls apart because you can't work with only one hand. The other will have been amputated because of pure stupidity. They'll have to sign up for unemployment and government assistance. *Then* what are you going to do?"

"Uh...technically, that's two questions..."

Aurora gave him a narrow-eyed look and planted her hands on her hips.

"The answer you're looking for is: *You're right, Aurora. I'm not going to do that.*" She squeezed his shoulder for emphasis. "Repeat after me."

Tim hung his head. "Okay. I'll take the day off and go see the damned hand doctor." He looked at Beau with a glare.

"Hey, don't look at me."

"She's *your* nurse."

"She's her own woman, though. Always has been." Beau looked at Aurora and a half smile crossed his face.

"Told you she was feistier than she used to be."

Tim said it as if it was a bad thing, but Beau could see her spirit rising every day.

"Let's get this show on the road so you can get to Truitt's Pharmacy for your antibiotics, and Keith can take you home." Aurora handed a printed prescription to Beau. "I wrote up the medications for you—antibiotics and some pain medicine."

"Can you put a sturdy dressing on him?"

Beau took the piece of paper from Aurora. His hand touched hers and lingered. Her gaze flashed to him, then she looked away.

"Oh, sure…" She cleared her throat and reached for a pair of gloves. "I'll put a dressing on you, Tim, but you'll have to come in tomorrow for me to change it. I'm sure Beau's going to want to see you again, too."

"Okay."

"Don't look so glum, Tim. You need a break. Fact is, I ran into your wife at Greg's Diner the other day. She looks like *she* needs a vacation too."

"You're right." He nodded and seemed to come to a decision. "Aurora. You give good advice. You should stick around and give us folks around here some more of it."

"Oh, Tim." She curved her hair behind her left ear. "I don't know…"

"Now, listen here," Tim said, and took her hand in his good one. "You may not realize this, but you've been missed around here."

"Yes, well… I've missed being around here, too." She turned, then winced, but covered it quickly. "Unfortunately Cathy's due back from maternity leave in a few days, so I'll be out of a job."

"Beau, can't you do something about that?"

"What would you suggest? Fire my nurse when she just had a baby?" Beau knew he'd said it a little more harshly than he'd intended. "Sorry, Tim. I'm in a bind, either way you look at it."

"Can't you keep them both on?"

"Not yet. Not enough business to justify hiring two nurses at the moment. We're getting there, but not right now."

"Well, shoot. That's too bad. But there has to be other jobs around, right? Maybe in town?" Tim's sympathy was genuine.

"I'm sure I'll figure something out. The right thing usually happens at the right time, don't you think?" Aurora patted Tim on the shoulder. "In the meantime, I'll call the hand doc in Johnstown and find out when he can see you."

Aurora nodded and placed a hand on her right hip as she left the room.

"Dammit." Tim spoke to Beau, but kept his gaze on their friend as she moved away.

"What?" Beau took a quick look out the door, but she'd disappeared.

"I just wish you could keep her on. She's too much fun to let walk out of here."

"I wish I could, too. But unless Cathy decides she's not coming back I have no choice but to let Aurora go," Beau said.

"Looks like you don't like that idea at all."

Tim eyed him closely. "And I don't mean just about the job."

"You're an observant man, Tim." A muscle twitched in Beau's jaw. He could feel it, and he was sure that Tim could see it. "Even if I *could* get her to stay, what have I got to offer her? I can't even give her a job! I've got too much baggage, Tim. I'm not sure I'm over…"

Was he over Julie? He'd certainly been happier lately than he had since her death. He shook his head and sighed.

"Anyway, she's got to *want* to stay. It's her plan to get her life back, and that life is in Virginia."

"It's your job to convince her. There are plenty of jobs in town, aren't there? She could get a job there until you've got enough business to hire her permanently."

Tim looked at him like that was the end of it, but it wasn't. Not by a long shot.

"It's an idea, but she hasn't said a word about finding another job."

"Have you asked her?"

Beau stared at the man. "Asked her what?"

"Asked her to stay?"

Beau shook his head. "It'd be selfish of me to ask her to stay. She needs to decide on her own."

With his good hand, Tim gave Beau a punch on the arm. "Have you lost your mind? The woman of your dreams is about to walk away from you and you're about to let her."

"What am I supposed to do? Kidnap her? Every time I try to talk to her lately something or someone interrupts." Beau shook his head, thinking of this very morning, when he'd made another attempt to talk to her. "As I said, she has to *want* to stay."

Tim leaned forward and peered right at Beau until his pulse jumped.

"Then give her a reason to stay."

Dumbfounded that his patient was giving him romantic advice, Beau simply stared at Tim for a few seconds. "Haven't you been listening? I can't offer her anything here."

"I'm not talking about the *job*, you dope."

"Neither am I…" Beau whispered.

Tim looked at him sympathetically. "You and Chloe. A family. That's what you can offer. A reason to stay."

"I can't expect her to take on a widower and a baby. I can't even guarantee it will work out, and I have Chloe to think of—it's not just me anymore."

Beau felt the tension in his neck creeping down into his shoulders and resisted the urge to give in to the pain of it. He cared for Aurora but, as broken as he was, could he offer her all she deserved? He wasn't going to beg her to stay. He had *some* pride left.

"Seriously? How long were you married?" Tim's eyes rounded wide, as if Beau had just said something monumentally stupid.

"Ten years. Why?"

"You told Julie you loved her once, didn't you?"

"Sure."

"Did you tell her more than that?"

"Of course. All the time."

"So, you think Aurora only wants or needs to hear it one time that you're interested in her? That you'd like her to stay here? If you want her to stay you need to find a way to talk to her, heart to heart. *Soon*. Before she gets it in her head to take a job in Alaska or something."

Tim stood. Apparently he'd come to the end of his wisdom for the day.

"Looks like you're good to go." Beau stood too. "Aurora will give you the paperwork and let you know when your next appointment is. Glad you came in, Tim. For the hand, I mean. The rest... I'm not so sure about."

"Me, too. I get a nail in the hand and the wife gets a vacation. Go figure." He shook his head as they walked to the reception area.

"It's the mysteries of life that keep it interesting, isn't it?"

"Yes, it is." Tim nodded toward Aurora, who sat at the desk with the phone to her ear. "And that's one fine mystery you ought to be solving right now."

"Tim—"

"You and I both know she belongs here. Her friends and family are here. Her history is here." Tim gave him the once-over. "So are you and Chloe."

Was Tim right? *Could* it work between them? Was he ready to move on after losing Julie? If Aurora stayed for him and things didn't work out, how awkward would that be for both of them?

"Maybe you're reading things that just aren't there."

Maybe he was too. Maybe he had been all along. Maybe his grief had hijacked his brain and led him down a path that really wasn't there.

"Back in the day, because you were so full of yourself and cheerleaders, you couldn't see what a great woman she is."

Beau took a look at her, perched on the edge of the new office chair he'd purchased for her while she chatted on the phone.

"I can see it now, but I can't… I'm not ready… I'm not sure what I can offer her."

"There is no perfect time. No one ever knows when they're ready. The loss of a loved one is always hardest on those left behind. But life goes on. We grieve and we move on. What I've learned about life, Beau, is it's never too late. If you're willing to take the chance. No matter what it is. No matter when it is. It could be a busted water pump, a lame horse, or a woman who needs you."

He clapped Beau on the shoulder with his good hand.

"Keith ought to be back in a few, so I'll finish up with Aurora and then you can take her to lunch or something."

Beau watched him chat with Aurora and her sunny smile for a few minutes, then salute as he left the clinic. There was some recurring pain behind that chipper face she presented to the world. He just hoped *he* hadn't contributed to it.

The bell overhead rang as Tim left and Beau cleaned the room, preparing it for the next patient. In this clinic he never knew what there would be going on at any given moment. He separated the used needles and placed them into the disposal container hanging on the wall.

"I can do that." Aurora made the offer. She'd entered the room, and he hadn't even heard her.

"No problem." He removed the bloody gauze and tossed it into the trash.

"So, it's past lunchtime. Are you going to head out?"

"We kind of lost our lunch hour with Tim, didn't we?" he asked.

"We did. That only gives us about twenty minutes to eat."

"That blows my plan, then."

"What plan was that?"

"I thought we could go out for lunch today."

They needed to talk—he knew that. Tim's words had gotten him thinking more than he already had been.

"Oh, no—not right before Brush Valley Day." Her eyes widened with concern. "There's too much to do. How about we go upstairs and make a few sandwiches or something? We can eat and go over the final touches of our plan for tomorrow. Oh, my, it's *tomorrow*."

She clasped her head with her hands, those blue eyes wide with worry.

"Relax, will you? It's just Brush Valley Day."

"No, it's *not*. It's the cornerstone of your entire business. I've put up notices on the community bulletin board online, on the community TV channel, on Craig's List, in every library in the county, and at Greg's Diner, Ramer's Pub and Grill, and even at the churches. We should be bombarded by people tomorrow."

"I can't believe it. You did all that?"

His eyes popped wide. How had she accomplished all that on such short notice? Was he so self-absorbed that he hadn't even seen what she was doing? Hadn't looked up to notice how wonderful she was and how well she fit into his office and his life?

Tim was right. He'd been too full of himself back then, but now he had no excuses.

"I did." A grin burst across her face. "I want to make a big splash tomorrow. It's the last community gathering before the weather turns and people will be out in droves. There's a steam and gas demonstration, old farm equipment on display...the Fosters are having a tractor-pull, and Karen Clever is having a dog wash for charity."

"What? How did you find all this out?" He stood, forgetting about cleaning the room. It could wait in light of the exuberance she had going on.

That beautiful grin returned. "Easy. Just hung out at the beauty shop for an afternoon and got all the gossip."

"Gossip?" Basing his practice on gossip was not what he'd been thinking.

She stepped closer. "On everyone."

That made him swallow. "What have you heard?"

"I'm not telling you." She pointed to the tray. "Finish up, wash up, and come up. By then I'll have some lunch made and I'll tell you everything."

With that declaration she left Beau with his mind boggled, his jaw dropped, and his heart hopeful. Tim was right. If he didn't at least try with Aurora then he didn't deserve her. He'd loved Julie with all his heart, but Aurora had made him smile again. He was a better person with her in his life. Even if it didn't last—as much as he wanted it to last forever—he and Chloe would be better off for their time with Aurora.

With renewed hope in his heart, he washed his hands at the galvanized metal sink and called to Daisy. "Let's go, girl. We've got some work to do. Make sure you act extra-cute, will you?"

After a hurried lunch and a quick return to the office Beau felt a renewed energy of spirit and heart. There was a chance for him to really make a go of things with Aurora, and the potential for building his practice at the clinic was growing by leaps and bounds with her ideas and her energy.

Aurora hung up the phone with a laugh that caught his attention. "What's going on?"

"Oh, that was Mrs. Kinsey. She made an

appointment for Monday." She shook her head and her eyes curled up at the corners.

As she looked at him Beau's heart contracted. He realized he was in love with her. He was a dope for not seeing it sooner and doing everything he could to convince her they were meant to be together.

"What for this time?" He was trying to focus on what she was saying, but his mind kept thinking that he loved her.

"She twisted her ankle at the Legion Hall dance—or maybe it was the Grange Hall. She said she was at both, so I'm a little confused about that. But, anyway, she wants you to check on it."

"Couldn't she come in today? We've got time."

"No." Aurora snorted a laugh and pressed the back of her hand to her nose and mouth as her eyes sparkled with mirth. "She's going to a seniors' Championship Twister tournament. She's in the finals!"

"Oh, my God!" Beau smiled, then gave a big laugh. "I'll bet she's going to twist more than her ankle *there*. You'd better set her a long appointment on Monday."

"I'm sure. I've booked her a double appointment."

Aurora shut down the computer and stood,

then put her hand on her right hip again with a muffled groan.

"Hip acting up again?"

"Yes. The chair is great—it's just the up and down stuff getting to me now." She nodded. "Since you did the last adjustment I've cut down on all of my medications, and now all I take is ibuprofen."

"You've made remarkable progress. You know that, right?" Somehow he resisted reaching out to her and taking her into his arms.

"I guess so, but I'm still not ready to swing from the rafters in the barn."

"How about before we leave today you let me adjust your back?"

"No." She waved him off and glanced away. "We have too much to do to get ready for tomorrow. It's not important right now."

"Aurora, it *can't* wait. You're more important than that stuff. *That's* what can wait, not you." Geez, she still didn't understand that yet.

"I don't want you to think I'm taking advantage of you because we work together." She gave a hesitant smile, indicating her insecurity about it.

"That's not possible—especially when I offer."

"It's not really that bad, Beau—"

"Hush." He placed his hands on her shoulders and slowly turned her around. "No one is more important to me than my child...and you."

He took a breath after saying the words that might end their relationship right now. Or they could be the words that solidified it.

"Please let me help you—let me see inside you, Aurora. When we talk about the tough stuff you shut down. I don't want that. I want to talk about it, bring it out into the light and see it for what it really is."

"What is it, then? *Really?*" Anger sparkled in those eyes. Anger that hid a massive pain.

"You've been hurt. Really hurt. You don't deserve to feel bad about it all, to carry the weight of others on your shoulders." Somehow he had to get through to her. Had to make her see how good they could be together. How good they were already.

"That's not it. You don't understand."

"That *is* it. I understand pain, and I understand anger, believe me."

"Beau. Please don't do this. We have other things to do right now." Tears brimmed in her eyes and two bright splotches appeared in her face.

Though she tried to resist and move away from him, he held her tight. This was the key to her torment, the reason she'd run and was still running now. Very few people saw who she was instead of seeing the things she did for them. Including him.

"I'm as guilty as anyone—and I'm here, right now, in front of you, saying I'm sorry. I know I've been focused on the clinic and getting things going, and you've done so many things for me and with Chloe. I don't know how I'd have gotten through these weeks without you. I'm also telling you now, Aurora Hunt, that I *see* you. I see who you are and you are one very awesome woman."

She gasped, the tension leaving her shoulders, and stared up at him, uncertainty in her eyes. "I don't want you to say those things."

For a second she dropped her gaze, then looked at him again. There it was. In her face. In her glistening eyes.

The fear. Fear drove her actions. Right now she was afraid she wasn't good enough. For him. For Chloe. For anything.

He cleared his throat and placed his hands on her shoulders, ensuring that she looked at him. It was now or never. If she didn't stay, then it was his own fault for not asking.

"We've skirted around this issue several times, but I'm going to say it officially. I want you to stay. Here in Pennsylvania. With me... and with Chloe."

* * *

She looked up at him, looked into those amazing green eyes. She couldn't find any deception, only pure honesty in his face, in his eyes, and tears filled her own eyes as she looked up at this man who had done his best to make a life for himself and his daughter, to create his business. And now he was trying to invite her into it.

Only *she* was resisting it. Only *she* was the one denying it was possible. Only *she* could see they wouldn't work.

"I don't know what to say…" That it wouldn't work because he was still in love with his dead wife?

"How about, *Yes, Beau, I'd love for you to adjust my hip, then we can get the rest of our work done*?"

At that, she allowed one corner of her mouth to curve upward as the intent of his words got to her. "Okay. I can go that far for now."

"The rest we'll work on—because you *are* a treasure, Aurora, whether you know it or not."

Once again, he held onto her shoulders until she looked into his eyes.

"There's more?"

"There's always more. Always going to be more. I'm serious about wanting you to stay with us."

The heat of his hands on her shoulders melted into her. She wanted this. Wanted him and baby Chloe.

"But why? There are so many things you don't know about me, about my life, about—"

"I'd like the chance to get to know all of those things, but if you don't stay we can't even try."

He took a deep breath and the energy in him changed. The vulnerability between them was nearly palpable.

"I know you're afraid. I am, too. But together we're so much stronger than we are alone, don't you think?"

That melted her resistance. That made her want to curl up by the fire with him for the rest of her life. But she'd worked so hard to leave this place, to build a life elsewhere—could she put it all aside and reach out to Beau the way he wanted? The way her heart desired?

"I… I'll…you've given me a lot to think about. Things I never considered when I got here."

Swallowing down the fear was hard, so very hard to do. But hadn't she told Tammie that she wasn't willing to give up just because it was hard?

Here was her defining moment.

Did she want Beau and Chloe more than she wanted to give in to the fear?

"I know. I never expected this either."

A tremor pulsed in his hands and she felt it inside her. He was as uncertain as she was, but at least he was willing to try. He was willing to give them a chance. To be a family together.

"We're good together, Aurora. You can see that, can't you?"

His eyes begged for her understanding. His face, the intensity of it, drew her closer as his hands drew her toward him.

"I want this, Beau. I want it so much. But I'm so afraid." She shook her head. It had to be said. The elephant in the room between them wasn't going away.

"Tell me—what are you afraid of? I can help you."

"I'm afraid of giving up everything I've worked for. My independence. I spent so long living by my parents' plan… When I finally broke free I never wanted to go back. But that stupid accident forced me down another path. One I didn't want but that led me to you. Now I feel so broken I'm worried I'm not good enough for you. What if I'm not as good as Julie? What if our relationship never measures up to what you had with her and we don't work? Then we'll *both* be hurt. And I don't want to risk our friendship."

He drew in a breath, as if she'd slapped him. In a way, she had. But it was the truth. It had had to be said.

He tried to talk, but no words came out of this throat.

"Wow. Just…wow."

He released her and paced across the room. With one hand he raked his hair back from his face, then faced her in a flash, shock and pain evident in his eyes.

"I had no idea, Aurora. No idea you thought this way."

Tears overflowed. "I'm so sorry, but I had to say it. I'm just so afraid what we have now isn't going to be as good as what you had with Julie, and you'll be disappointed, and angry…"

Her hands trembled and she clasped them together against her middle as she said the final words of fear that lingered in her heart. The final words that could end her relationship with Beau permanently.

"I'm afraid to lose everything I've worked for. To lose our friendship. My heart has been battered and broken so much already." A ragged breath huffed out of her throat. "I love you and Chloe, and nothing would make me happier than to be with you, but I'm afraid I'll never measure up to what you had. And I'm not sure I'm prepared to take the risk."

Without a word, Beau strode past her and out the door.

Brush Valley Day arrived very early for Aurora. She'd set her alarm for five a.m. as she had so much to do before the festival. Somehow, in these weeks she'd been working with Beau, she'd begun to claim some ownership of the little clinic in her rural home town. Today she wanted to show it off. And not just to help increase Beau's business. If she were being honest about it, she was proud of what they'd accomplished in such a short time.

That thought made her pause.

They'd definitely accomplished a lot in the office and in renewing their friendship. Was she wrong to have balked at Beau's words last night? Why could she throw herself wholeheartedly into her job, yet when it came to happiness she wasn't willing to take the risk?

For weeks she'd been excited about today, but now she wasn't as eager as she'd expected. The conversation they'd had last night had cut severely into her joy. Last night things had gone all wrong. The pain in his face had been caused by *her* words and she wished she'd never said anything.

The ache in her heart wasn't going to go away until they talked again. If he even showed up. If he ever talked to her again.

She needed to focus on what was right in front of her. It was the only thing she could do—carry on with the plan. It might be the last thing she could do for Beau.

She staked out a choice location close to the chicken stand. Ever the opportunist, she thought she could hand out fliers on esophageal reflux and indigestion while people were in the midst of a digestive flare-up.

Though she thought of all those things, the joy of the day had been dampened and the sun was hardly above the horizon.

Scanning the street for his vehicle, she sighed. If she and Beau were at odds, this was going to be a very long day.

Finally Beau's SUV backed up into the space beside her car and she hurried over to him.

"I'm so glad you decided to come." Trying not to panic, she took a breath and hoped her deodorant was going to live up to its all-day reputation.

"Why wouldn't I? We've been planning this for weeks."

"Well, after last night… I thought you might… not come."

"Never even considered it." Beau squeezed one of her shoulders. "Let's get moving, shall we?"

Beau looked at his watch and gave her that grin of his. There was just a hint of the pain from last night in his eyes. Apparently he'd decided to set it aside for today. For right now, for the sake of the festival, she'd go with it. Who knew what kind of relationship they'd have after that? If any.

"Well. Okay. I'm anxious about getting things set up."

And a lot of other things. She shot him another glance, but he maintained his composure, his demeanor, and she relaxed a little. Maybe they could get through the day on an equal footing before he told her to get out of his life.

"If you can help me with the table, we'll get everything rolling."

"Lead the way."

They worked together to get the display and the sun shade up before the first events of the day began. For a few hours they tag-teamed, alternating offering flu shots and blood pressure checks, taking down contact information and handing out fliers.

"Wow. Not too many takers," Aurora said,

heartily disappointed in the number of people who'd stopped by their booth. "I've only had three BP checks and six flu shots." She plopped down into her chair and shoved her hair out of her face. "This is discouraging. I thought more people would be interested in us. I mean, you. The clinic."

"Oh, just wait until after lunch. People will settle down then, get something to eat, work on their indigestion, then come over to see if we have any antacids."

Beau was looking at the situation a different way than she did.

"We don't *have* any antacids. I never thought of that!"

Beau fished around in a box beneath the table, shook a giant bottle of antacids and sat it in front of her. "We do now. In a moment of clarity I grabbed some from the pharmacy on the way over."

"Oh, you think you're so smart, don't you?"

"I try to be."

Secretly pleased at his thoughtfulness, she felt a warmth pulse in her chest. Could they really do this together? This thing they were already doing?

Before she had any time to mull over that idea, there was a new arrival at their table.

CHAPTER TWELVE

As Beau had predicted, the afternoon saw a flurry of increased activity at their little booth. People were looking for information on a variety of illnesses and there was renewed interest in flu shots.

"I've started an email list for people to subscribe to your newsletter."

"I don't have a newsletter."

"You do now."

"Awesome." Beau patted his stomach. "The smell of that chicken is driving me nuts. How about I go get us some lunch?"

"I haven't had it in years, so I'm overdue."

The first piece of smoky barbecue chicken to hit her tongue brought back so many memories for Aurora that she closed her eyes and squealed.

"Too hot?"

She shook her head.

"Must be good, then."

She nodded her head and silently chewed as memories assaulted her from every direction.

So many things that one bite of food gave to her. Memories of family excursions to the fair, memories of her teenage years, going on dates to the fair, or hanging out with her friends. Memories assaulted her, overwhelmed her. Friends she'd lost track of, family who were no longer with them, events she'd missed.

Pain suddenly hit her in the gut as she chewed. Tears filled her eyes, then overflowed.

"What's wrong? That bad?"

She choked down the piece of food and opened her watery eyes to Beau, now stooped in front of her. "No. I've missed *so* much." She hiccuped in a breath. "Being gone. I've missed it here, but I'd convinced myself I didn't belong here, that my life was elsewhere."

"One bite of chicken told you that?"

"Yes." Again and again memories of years past trickled into her brain, and she placed her hand on his strong shoulder, needing a connection with him right now. "I ran away, and I kept running and running, didn't I?"

"Yes, you did, but you had reasons for it, right?"

"I did. I had to go. I had to get out of here. I had to find my life, to make my life somewhere else—or at least that's what I thought at the time. But now I just don't know."

"You did. Now it's time for you to come home, Aurora. Come home to the people who love you, and miss you, and want to see you here every day." He stayed in front of her, with not a care about the people flowing around them.

"How can I do that when I've hurt people, cut them out by leaving? My friends. My family. I don't want to hurt anyone else. Especially you." She placed her hand on his face. "I've hurt you, and I keep doing it, don't I?"

"Shh, Aurora." He pulled her close and hugged her. "You carry the weight of the world on your shoulders, and you don't have to. Just be *you*, and everything will be fine."

The reassurance in his voice comforted her in the moment.

"When you said you weren't prepared to take the risk you shocked the hell out of me. Everything you've done with your life—building your career from scratch in a new state, returning here and starting again, all the chances you took… But I wasn't worth the risk. I wasn't ready for that and it was a slap in the face."

"I'm so sorry, Beau."

"You were right." He nodded and held her gaze. "But you were wrong, too."

"Er…what?"

"We *are* worth the risk. We're already better than I ever could have imagined. I loved Julie, and I always will, but I'm *in love* with you."

A few seconds passed before the impact of his words sank in. "Really?" She sat bolt upright in the chair and nearly knocked Beau over.

"Yes, really." He cupped her face in his hands and drew her closer for a hard kiss. "I've been trying to figure out a way to keep you here and the answer was as simple as being honest with myself and with you."

"Beau, are you sure? I mean, are you really ready for this? What about Chloe?"

"She's already fond of you and has accepted you, so with time I'm sure she'll love you as much as I do." He cleared his throat and glanced away. "So, Aurora Hunt, will you stay in Brush Valley, with me, with Chloe, and someday be my wife?"

"Beau..." The word was a breath on the air, a sigh from her soul. Everything was in that one word. "Yes, I'll stay. I don't know what I'll do for work, but I won't leave. I won't leave you and Chloe. I love you both so much."

"We'll find a job for you somewhere until the clinic is busy enough for two nurses. I just don't want you to go. I want to give us a chance."

"I want that, too."

Lunging from the chair, she launched herself into Beau's arms and hung onto him.

Someone nearby cleared his throat loudly and a familiar voice interrupted them. "Hey, you two. Just who I was looking for."

Aurora pulled back and wiped her eyes with the heels of her hands, hoping she hadn't smeared her mascara.

"Tim!" Beau stood in front of Aurora, giving her a minute to catch her breath while he still trembled from the effort to control his emotions in the moment. "What can I do for you?"

"I got my dressing all torn up."

He held up his hand. It was *not* the pristine white dressing that he'd left the office with. It was falling off and streaked with smudges of who knew what?

"Come over here before Aurora sees it." Beau led him to the opposite side of the tent. "You just can't stay out of trouble, can you, Tim?"

"You know me, don't you, Beau?" Tim gave a laugh and sat on the chair and began to unwrap the dressing by himself. "I got a new horse who needs some extra attention. Got my dressing wrapped up in the bridle. He spooked, then we both ran around the corral like maniacs until the wrapping tore away. It's all dirty, and I knew Aurora would probably give me hell, so I decided to man up and come to you before she finds out and yanks me around by the ear."

"I wouldn't do that, Tim Verner."

There she stood with her hands on her hips, looking like she would do exactly that, and Beau allowed one side of his mouth to curl up. She was a force to be reckoned with, and he loved her with all his heart. In that moment, as he stood there watching her give his patient a hard time, the broken pieces of his heart were melding back together again.

Yes, he would always love Julie. She'd given him the best piece of herself before she died, and he would honor her and their love all the remaining days he spent on earth. But the earth-bound man needed to move on, *had* to move on. With Aurora by his side, he knew he could do it. He could have a good life, raise his daughter, and maybe have a few more running around.

"You most certainly would." Tim barked out a laugh. "I remember you yanking Beau around by the ear in geometry class when you bombed a test and he put it up on the bulletin board. You grabbed him by the ear and had him on his knees until he apologized." He slapped his good hand on his leg. "I'll never forget that."

"Neither will I." Beau rubbed his ear, which suddenly burned from the memory.

Aurora's eyes went wide and she clapped a

hand over her mouth. "I totally forgot about that." She stood upright, like every stern teacher they'd ever had. "But I'm going to remember it now if you really did what you *said* you did." She gave him a stern look. "Thanks for the refresher, Tim. Now let me see what damage you did while wrangling a wild horse."

She brushed aside Beau's hands, obviously recovered from the bout with her emotions, but her gaze kept darting toward him. That was good.

He watched Aurora give Tim an earful about bacteria and flesh-eating staph, gangrene, and all manner of ills that would befall him should he choose to ignore her instructions. *Again.*

"Okay. Okay. I'll behave myself." He shook his head and looked at her sheepishly from under the rim of his dusty cowboy hat.

"Your definition of that differs a lot from mine." Aurora snorted and added an extra layer of tape, giving him a dose of the stink eye as she did so. "Don't get it dirty—or I'll be calling your wife to watch you closer."

"Please don't do that." Tim squirmed a little in his seat. "That's really unnecessary."

"Then behave yourself. The longer you keep irritating the wound, the longer it will take to heal."

"I know. I *know*."

"Then *do* it. What you resist, persists. Have you ever heard that?"

"No. But I get it." Shaking his head, he widened his eyes briefly. "Boy, do I get it."

"Okay. Lecture over." She gave him another look, watching to see if her words had really sunk into his brain. "For now. Don't screw this up before you even get to see the hand surgeon."

"Beau? Can you *do* something about her?" Playful as ever, Tim teased him.

"What? Me? No way. Not touching that one." Beau held his hands up like he was facing a rattlesnake.

It turned into a good-natured argument about who was going to do what. This little moment was just the kind of fun Aurora needed. Another person from her past reinforcing how much she was needed here. How much she was wanted here. Not just because of him and how good they were together.

"Excuse me. Is this a bad time?" A woman stood a few feet away, hesitating.

"This is a perfect time." Beau stood and greeted her, glad that people were still stopping by for a variety of reasons. "I'm Dr. Gutterman. What can I do for you?"

"I was interested in getting a flu shot."

"Great. My nurse Aurora is in charge of those, so I'll place you in her capable hands."

After Aurora had finished up, he approached her.

"I never could have done this without your input and help, Aurora. *Never*."

"Oh, it wasn't that much. Really…"

She dropped her gaze as a flush colored her neck and face. Though she tried to brush off the compliment, he could see that she was pleased.

"Just take the compliment and my gratitude for what they are."

"What *are* they?"

"Sincere."

"Beau…"

Now she met his gaze, her eyes glistening with the happiness that he'd wanted to see there for a long time. Knowing he'd put it there pleased him. He'd like to spend all his days looking for that ray of sunshine in her eyes.

"It's true."

He leaned over to kiss her cheek, then turned as he heard a familiar little voice. The squeal let him know who was coming.

"Chloe!"

He greeted the toddler with all the enthusiasm that Aurora expected to see—had missed seeing in the men in *her* family. What was so different about him? He was certainly manly, masculine and strong, but he had a soft side when it came to his daughter. It was lovely to see and something in her heart turned.

Was she really looking at this man who'd been her friend for years in the right light? Could he really be a partner to her in work and in her heart? Letting him in could risk heartache again, for both of them, but anything in life that was worth having was worth taking a risk on, wasn't it?

As the thrumming in her chest made her breathing tight she watched as Beau clasped Chloe in his hands, then gave her a little toss in the air, and she knew she was done for. There was no way she was leaving Beau and Chloe.

Nothing was as important to her as they were.

The baby squealed, delighted with the play. Then Beau tucked her against his side, pressed a kiss to her chubby little cheek. The pain in Aurora's chest burst and tears filled her eyes as she watched the man she'd fallen in love with play with his child.

The sun continued to move westward, casting the man in a bronze glow. His shoulders looked broader, his hips leaner, his legs longer, and when he turned to face her with a grin he was more handsome, his hair more golden blond, and his skin glowed in a way she'd never noticed.

When he looked at her that way, with pure joy in his eyes, her heart cramped in her chest and her knees felt weak and trembling.

She was completely, totally, outrageously in love with Beau Gutterman. Hopelessly in love with him.

As he approached, Chloe reached out to Aurora and her heart beat a little faster again. Tears pricked her eyes at the little girl's plea, and she took Chloe from Beau.

"How's Chloe doing today?" She smiled and gave her a kiss.

"She's been a good baby all day, but somehow she knew it was time to see her daddy," said Dolly, Beau's mother.

The woman turned and approached Aurora with an assessing look on her face. Her eyes were the same vivid green as Beau's, and it was obvious where his looks came from.

"You must be Aurora?"

"Yes, I am." With her hands full of baby, she couldn't shake Dolly's hand, so she nodded. "It's been a long time, hasn't it?"

"Oh, yes. I do recall meeting you once or twice when you kids were in school. Beau tells me you've been a godsend to him at the office."

"He does?"

She cast a quick look at the man whose face was unreadable at the moment. Aurora couldn't tell anything of what he was thinking or feeling from the way his eyes were guarded and the firm set of his mouth. All moisture left her mouth as she stared at him.

After a short visit, Dolly took Chloe and placed her in her stroller. "I think I'll take her home before the fireworks get started. They'll be too loud for her."

"Good idea." Beau leaned over and pressed a kiss to his mother's cheek. "Thanks for taking her today."

"It is a joy. She's a good baby, and I love having her."

"You have to tell me, though, if she gets too much for you."

Dolly Gutterman pulled herself upright and raised one brow at her son. "Are you trying to tell me that I'm getting too old to handle a baby?"

A flash of a grin took over Beau's face for a few seconds before he controlled his expression. "No, ma'am. I'd never do that."

"Good. Having a baby around makes me feel younger every day." Her bright look was taken over by a sad grief for a few seconds, as Dolly looked at her granddaughter, who was falling asleep right in front of them. "I just wish things were different. That she had a mom to love her, too."

"She will. I promise." He placed a hand on Dolly's arm and gave a little squeeze. "I'll give you a call when we're all wrapped up here."

"Okay. By then I'm sure she'll be asleep. She can stay overnight. I don't mind at all."

"If you don't mind… Aurora and I have some things to finish up and it could get late."

"Call me in the morning."

She raised her face to his and he kissed his mother on the cheek, then kissed Chloe and watched as they moved away.

Aurora had stood transfixed, watching the conversation between Beau and Dolly.

"Beau!"

A feminine voice called to him, and both he and Aurora turned to look.

"Don't leave yet."

"Cathy?"

Beau placed his hands on his hips and grinned at the woman coming their way. A baby was strapped to her chest and her husband kept pace with them as he toted a diaper bag.

"You look *fabulous*." The awe in his voice was almost tangible. Beau eased the blue cover away from the baby's face. "He's beautiful!"

Despite herself, Aurora was drawn closer to the new family too. This was the baby that she and Beau had delivered together her first day here.

"Oh, he's a beauty, for sure," Aurora said, and the pain, the hurt in her chest dissipated as the baby shifted position and yawned, then settled down again. "How are you doing?"

"I feel great." The look of adoration Cathy cast on her baby was pure bliss. "He's a good baby, and sleeps most of the night."

"That's a miracle in itself," Aurora said, knowing that not *every* baby slept through the night.

"I'm so glad you stopped by." Beau stretched around her and shook hands with Ron, her husband. "Are you ready to come back to work yet?"

Aurora held her breath. Her future rode on the answer to that question. Moisture broke out on her palms and her tongue felt like it was stuck to the roof of her mouth. Her heart, which had just been quiet, now thrummed with anxiety. She waited for Cathy's answer.

"Oh, that's something I wanted to talk to you about." She looked at her husband, then a grin erupted on her face. "While I've been off, Ron got a promotion, and now I don't have to work at *all*!"

Cathy practically glowed as she announced

that her dream of becoming a full-time wife and mother had actually come true.

"We never thought we could do it on one income, but now I can stay home with the baby and Ron can bring home the bacon."

Beau cast a quick glance at Aurora, then faced Cathy again. "I'm thrilled for you. You'll have to bring him in for his first round of shots soon, and all that fun stuff."

"I will." Cathy faced Aurora. "I also wanted to thank you both for helping when I went into labor. You saved our lives." Tears overflowed on Cathy's face. "I'm sorry. My hormones are a wreck."

She wiped her face with the baby's blanket.

"Come here." She hugged them both as well as she could with the baby on her chest. "When I come in to visit, I expect that waiting room to be full."

"I hope you're right." Beau hugged her back.

"With everything that I've heard around town, you're going to be busier than ever. This isn't something I anticipated happening for a long time. But with a new baby, I just want to stay home and rock him, and watch every time he does something. It's so new and wonderful and scary all at the same time."

"You'll be fine, Cathy. You'll both be fine. If I could be a new dad and take care of Chloe with…with everything that went on, you can do it for sure."

His voice cracked as he spoke and Aurora knew he was remembering how Julie had died, and her heart ached for him.

After they'd left, Beau turned to her and grinned. "The job's yours if you want it." He paused. "*Do* you want it?"

With a squeal she wrapped her arms around his shoulders. "Of *course* I want it!"

Beau's arms clasped her tight and the tremor in his muscles reached her heart.

"There's nothing else I want more."

They stowed all the supplies in their vehicles, then Beau faced Aurora and held on to her shoulders as the night deepened and the crickets began their nightly tunes.

"Will you stay with me? I want to hold you tonight." His breathing was fast and hard, matching her own. "Chloe's staying with my mom, and we can have some adult time together."

"Beau…" Without her consent, her hands moved up to clasp his shirt in her fists. Pulses of desire filled her as she eased closer to him.

"We've come so far in our lives alone." He pressed a kiss to her forehead. "I want to get to know you all over again. And again. And again."

"I do, too." Any remaining pieces of ice and

protection surrounding her heart rapidly melted beneath Beau's warmth and his words.

Without another word he swooped down and kissed the living daylights out of her. If that kiss didn't tell her how he felt, then nothing would.

He pulled back. "Aurora, I love you. I love you so much." He cupped her face and waited until she looked up at him with watery eyes.

"I love you, too. You mean so much to me, and I can't stay here without being with you and Chloe. It would kill me."

For a few moments they stood in the twilight, just holding each other, shaking and trembling with need, trying to hold on to these new feelings, new realizations, and new possibilities for them together.

In a flash, Beau brought her against him again and squeezed her. "We're going to be great together. We're going to be a family. The three of us."

"Kiss me. Kiss me like you're never going to let me go."

Reaching up, she guided his mouth to hers. She parted her lips to him and ached with need as he devoured her, driving desire up to the surface.

They explored each other and Beau pressed her against the car, pressing his hips against hers, letting her know in no uncertain terms of his desire for her.

"Let's go. I need you, Aurora. I need you *now*."

He dipped and took her mouth with his again, then they both jumped as lights flashed overhead and seconds later came the resounding boom of fireworks.

"Oh!" Aurora looked overhead at the spiraling lights streaming back to earth. "I'd forgotten about this."

"I hadn't. I knew there were going to be fireworks tonight," Beau said, but he wasn't looking up. He was looking straight at her.

"Oh, really?" That made her smile. "Fireworks?"

"Yes, there are *always* fireworks when we're together." Beau took a breath and pressed his forehead against hers. "Then you'll stay? Stay with me tonight, every night, and build a life with me?"

The fear and the vulnerability in his voice broke her heart. They'd both had their share of tragedies, but together she knew they could build a life, build a business and build on the love they already had for each other.

"I'll stay and love you forever."

EPILOGUE

One year later

FALL WAS AURORA'S favorite time of the year in Pennsylvania. Every year was special, with the leaves in full color, but this year was extraspecial.

Today she was approaching the lake just outside of town, and she admired the afternoon sun glistening on the surface, sparkling and adding a little magic to the day. Leaves scattered by the wind clattered across the road onto the grass and swirled past the crowd gathered there.

Since she'd woken this morning her heart had been in overdrive, and as the horse-drawn wagon she was riding in arrived she felt it hammer in her chest.

The crowd of people—friends and family, some who were both—were gathered at the edge of the lake and waiting for her to arrive.

"Whoa!" Tim pulled on the reins and the horses slowed to a stop.

After getting down, Aurora looked for Beau. There he was, under an arch at the water's edge, looking strong and handsome and so very loving as he waited for her to arrive.

The last year had been a whirlwind of love, of blending two families, and of her realizing that what she'd needed had been in Brush Valley all along.

"Thank you, Tim." She leaned up and kissed his clean-shaven cheek.

"You're welcome." He cleared his throat. "You're a beautiful bride, Aurora, and I'm grateful that you're my friend, too."

Tears choked her throat as she took the few steps toward her mother, who stood proud and beautiful, wearing a peach-colored dress that mirrored Aurora's gown.

"Are you ready to walk me down the aisle?" Aurora asked.

"You're sure this is what you want?" Sally's voice was choked with emotion.

After a quick look at Beau, she nodded. "Absolutely. Today is the best day of my life."

"I just wish your father were here."

Aurora looked overhead at the bright blue sky and at the way a light breeze teased the trees. "He's here, Mom. He's here."

In minutes she held Beau's hand and the words were spoken that would join them together as partners, friends, soul mates and as family.

Then Beau's lips were on hers and the crowd around them applauded. Beau hugged her with one arm and took Chloe with his other, and the three of them stood together, united as one family, one unit, one love.

* * * * *

*If you enjoyed this story,
check out these other great reads
from Molly Evans*

*SAFE IN THE SURGEON'S ARMS
HER FAMILY FOR KEEPS
SOCIALITE...OR NURSE IN A MILLION?
CHILDREN'S DOCTOR, SHY NURSE*

All available now!